Sulfurings:
Tales from Sodom & Gomorrah

Biblical Legends Anthology Series

Edited by
Allen Taylor
Published By
Garden Gnome Publications

Copyright © 2012 by
Garden Gnome Publications
Second Printing, December 2017
Third Printing, August 2023
Cover art
by Alexandre Rito

ISBN: 13:978-1540836090
ISBN-10:1540836096
ISBN: 979-8-9900498-0-2

All works included herein are fictitious. Any characters resembling actual persons, living or dead, or businesses, events, animals, creatures, and settings resembling real world businesses, events, animals, creatures, and settings are purely coincidental, except of course Sodom and Gomorrah and their legendary inhabitants. If any of them have a beef with the way authors in this anthology have handled their memories, they can take it up with the authors. The garden gnomes are merely middlemen.

DEDICATION

This anthology is dedicated to anyone who has ever sulfured.

CONNECT WITH THE GNOMES

The garden gnomes would sincerely like to connect with you at our social media outposts. Please, drop on by!

Follow our editor on Twitter, Hive, and Paragraph.

Table of Malcontents

ALPHA

By Allen Taylor

Years ago, when I conceptualized the Biblical Legends Anthology Series (BLAS), I had no idea how they would be received. I also had no idea what quality of writing I would see or the nature of the content. I'm quite pleased.

Garden of Eden, the first and the smallest of the three anthologies published thus far, set the expectations for *Sulfurings: Tales from Sodom & Gomorrah*, which took a different turn. The apocalyptic flavor of this anthology won't sit well with everyone, but for readers who like this kind of literature, it should hit the spot. The writers included herein caught the spirit of what I was attempting to do with the anthology, and I'm thankful for them all.

Selling at physical events has allowed me to gauge reader reactions in a way that can't be done online. Generally, I see three reactions:

1. Enthusiastic acceptance;
2. Gross rejection, or shock;
3. Or the general assumption that because they're based on Bible stories, they are *de facto* "Christian" literature.

I'm thankful for the first type of reader, and the second type isn't my audience. The third type of reader, however, falls into two categories: Christians who expect the stories to present a Christian point of view and non-Christians who do the same.

While some stories in *Sulfurings* are written by Christian authors, some are not. I didn't ask writers about their backgrounds. It didn't occur to me to do so because I was looking for good stories with a speculative twist on the biblical narratives. We weren't reinventing theology, after all. We were reimagining literature.

Readers may notice some of the details in certain stories are inaccurate, or they may disagree with a writer's interpretation of the biblical drama. On the other hand, readers may find some interesting explorations of sin, redemption, righteousness, God's wrath, and related biblical themes. These themes may be explored even as events stray from the biblical storyline. In other cases, the themes are explored satirically.

During the submissions process, as editor and as publisher, I made only two stipulations. First, stories must be set in Sodom or Gomorrah at the time of their destruction or shortly thereafter. Second, I asked writers not to include biblical characters in their stories.

I was so pleased with the stories I received that I was inspired to write one of my own. It's included in this anthology despite the usual flak editors receive for publishing themselves.

Changes in this second edition begin and end with author bios. The stories have not changed. I requested that authors update their bios for the second printing of *Sulfurings*. Most added publishing credits or changed their credits to more recent ones. Some didn't respond at all. One author unexpectedly announced his transgender status. In our present day of cancel culture and protest for protest's sake, that story could invite controversy for reasons other than its content. I didn't think it would be fair to ask the author to edit his bio, nor would it be fair to pull his story based on some moral sensibility, whether mine or someone else's. Some readers may question my judgment or accuse me of "endorsing" transgenderism. Be that as it may, that author's story stands on its own merit. His lifestyle choices are subject to God's judgment (as are mine and everyone else's), and I'm not God.

I'm delighted that writers and readers alike may be driven to the Bible to read the text where the original stories can be found, and I hope the anthologies honor the original stories in some way even if individual literary creations stray far afield.

I do not wish to linger any more on sentimental aphorisms and self-important atta-boys. So, without further ado, I'll turn it over to the writers themselves and bid you happy reading.

FLASH FICTIONS

AND A CHILD SHALL LEAD

Rie Sheridan Rose

The night before the sky fell, Rebecca pleaded with Malachi not to leave the house. He didn't listen. He never listened.

His friends were going to Lot's home—there were new men in town that the Sodomites wanted to "welcome" to the neighborhood. She knew what that meant. She hated it. Why couldn't the men of Sodom stay home with their families? If it was just for the sex ... she was willing to learn if it would keep him home.

When the wailing started outside the earthen walls of the little two room house, she felt her way to the door. Blindness was a burden she accepted as the Lord's will. The portal opened to a warm, humid night. She stepped out onto the street, one hand on the lintel of the door.

"Malachi!" she called anxiously. "Malachi, where are you?" Her heart pounded in her chest. The screaming and crying were coming closer. She could make out dozens of individual voices in the mayhem. Was Malachi's one of them? She wasn't sure.

"Rebecca!" Malachi's voice was odd ... whimpering. She'd never heard him cry before.

"Here, Malachi. What is it?" she asked, reaching into the darkness.

He fell into her arms. "I can't see." He sobbed like a child.

So, the shoe was on the other foot now, was it? Now Malachi was experiencing what she had known from birth, and it was terrifying him. She had always thought him so very strong.

***

When the sun peeked through the window the next morning, Rebecca felt it on her face as she always did. Malachi was curled beside her, having finally cried himself to sleep after midnight.

She rose to her feet without disturbing him. Time to fetch water from the well. Breakfast would not cook itself.

She felt for her water pot and then started across the square to the well. As she walked the path she knew by heart, she felt the sting of something against her cheek. There was the smell of sulfur in the air.

The sound of screaming filled the air around her. Malachi! He was alone and helpless. She needed to get back to him ....

She started back toward the little house where she had been happy with Malachi. He had treated her well—as well as he knew how.

More stinging sulfur hit her face and hands. Her linen shift was scorched in a dozen places. Her bare feet stumbled as she stepped on hot patches of sulfur on the dusty path.

She found the house more by luck than anything else, falling through the doorway on her hands and knees. They had to get out!

Her panic subsided. They should be safe in the house, shouldn't they? Four stout clay walls and a sturdy thatch roof ... But the stench of sulfur was already thick in the inside of the house. The rain of burning sulfur would catch the thatch on fire if they stayed.

"Malachi." She fumbled through her clothing chest, feeling for something that could provide some extra protection. Her winter cloak ... the extra blanket ... not a great deal of help, but better than nothing. She wrapped the cloak around her head.

"Malachi." She shook out the blanket and felt her way to the bed. "Wake up. We need to get out of here. Hurry!"

He mumbled in his sleep and pushed her away.

"Get up! We have to leave. Please, Malachi! I can't do it without you."

"Leave me alone. Just let me die."

"I need you."

"For what? I can't see any more than you can. The only reason I took you to wife is that you wouldn't see the actions I wanted hidden. Now, I can't see either. So how can I help you do anything? I just want to die in peace."

The smell of sulfur was getting stronger. There was no time to argue.

"I am leaving." She laid the extra blanket over him. "I will be back when the rain stops."

She took up her staff and stumbled out of the house. The screams were echoing from all sides. She cocked her head. Was that Joshua crying? He was only five. She moved toward the sound of the child's cries. "Joshua! Joshua, where are you?"

"Rebecca, I'm here."

She felt his arms go around her waist and knelt beside him. "What do you see, Joshua?"

Through his hiccoughing sobs, he managed to say, "The sky is raining fire. Yellow fire that stinks. It is tearing away the buildings."

"We need to get out of here, Joshua. Can you help me?"

"I think so."

"Where is your family?"

"Father was sick this morning. He wouldn't get out of bed."

Blind like Malachi, she bet. They had pushed too far the night before. Was this retaliation for whatever the men had done?

"And Mother ..." His voice caught, then continued, "Mother was burned up."

She hugged the child close. "I'm sorry, Joshua. I will take care of you if you take care of me."

He took her hand. "I see a way that isn't too burned."

"Lead me out of here."

The rain hissed around them as Rebecca and Joshua stumbled along, jostled by other fleeing Sodomites. The sulfur was burning their lungs as the flame seared their feet and clothes.

The fire was taking its toll. They couldn't go any further.

"I see a cave in the rocks," Joshua cried excitedly. He tugged her hand, and she followed without question, too tired to question.

She was disoriented. Where was the house? Was Malachi all right?

Joshua dragged her into the rocks. The cave was barely enough for the two of them.

She sat, back to the solid wall of the cave, and took Joshua into her lap. Her sensitive fingers explored the boy for burns. He seemed relatively unhurt.

"Your hair is all burnt up," Joshua said with a tired giggle.

Her hand went to her head. Yes, there were clumps of singed curls. But it would grow back. Could the same be said for Sodom?

"What do you see, Joshua?"

"The town is falling down. All the houses are squashed. People are lying down, too."

He lay his head against her shoulder. "Everything is going away, Rebecca."

"We're safe here," she said, hoping it was true. Sometimes it was better not to see the world around you. At least you didn't see it sneaking up on you.

Joshua was snoring softly, finding solace in sleep.

She let her head fall back against the rock. "Please, my Lord … let us be safe here."

She slipped into sleep herself … and the Lord answered her prayer.

ABEL

Melchior Zimmermann

Abel was breathing in great gasps, a ragged sound coming from his throat. The sulfurous air scorched his lungs. He coughed up congealed blood, dark red drops clinging to his parched lips. Yellow smoke billowed around the heap of rubble that had once been his home. He looked around frantically, searching for a sign of his family.

A broken doll, squashed between rocks. A broken table, its wooden remains still smoldering. A white piece of fabric that had once belonged to his mother's dress. Nothing was moving. The only sound he could hear was the slow crackling of the burning furniture.

Abel remembered the days spent within the walls of his home. The meals he had shared with his family and his friends. The work he had done in the smithy, under the supervision of his stern father. The festivals he had enjoyed in town with his friends. The kisses he had shared with the girls and boys from his neighborhood. Now all that was left was a smoldering, stinking wasteland of brimstones and toxic fumes.

In one day, his life had been torn asunder. The fiery stones had rained from the sky, burning their way through stone and flesh alike, scorching the earth. All that was left was burnt and blackened soil. Never again would life sprout out of it. Never again would a palace be built in this place. Never again would goods be made, trade be conducted, lives born, or deaths honored.

Stumbling over crumbling stones, Abel wandered through the wasteland. Each breath was more painful than the last. Each step brought him closer to death. He could hear the wailing sounds of his fellows, the agonizing cries of the damned few that had not yet died. He could feel the blood dripping into his lungs, filling them up, and casting out the foul air he breathed. In the mad cackling of the flames, for the first time in his life, he could hear the voice of God.

IDBASH

Melchior Zimmermann

It had been a moon ago that Idbash had last set eyes upon the great city-state of Sodom. Every month, he would come to the market to sell his wares and buy what he might need from the other merchants. If life on the plains was hard, the soil was fertile, and trade with the city-states allowed even a humble farmer like himself to make a living.

Idbash had never found much joy in the rites of Sodom. But he knew that wherever he went to sell his crops, he would need to bow to the customs of his customers. And even if the people of Sodom might have stranger customs than the shepherds of the mountains, they also paid a better price for his wares.

He was setting up his stand once more, in the same spot as the other times, exchanging idle barter with the neighboring merchants, when he heard a loud rumble coming from above. The sky had been a clear blue when he had set out that morning, but during the day, dark clouds had gathered. Afraid a storm was brewing, he glanced up.

Blazing stones of fire were falling from the clouds. A hailstorm from hell, they blasted apart the mighty buildings of the city, burning their way through the inheritance of centuries past. Idbash turned around to look at his fellows just in time to see them melt under the hellfire unleashed from heaven. Screams of women and children rent the air as the divine purge melted the city, tearing life from limb. The earth screeched in protest, bursting asunder under the bombardment of retribution. People shouted and ran, but the sulfurous fires of God found them wherever they hid.

For the first time in his life, Idbash knew what fear was. Not the petty feeling that might overcome you before first confessing your love to a pretty girl. Not the mild discomfort you might feel when faced with a wolf, or any other beast. No, the fear he felt was the fear of God. The fear you know when all around you life is fighting, and life is losing, and you know that, sooner or later, you will go the same way. No matter if you stay or run, death will come from you and rob you of everything you hold dear, and all you can do is wait.

Whether it was hours or seconds, Idbash did not know. He stood still, next to his cart, while the rain of fire fell around him. He saw the men he had done business with being torn apart. He saw their wives bursting into flames, babes held close to their breasts. Over and over, he saw death and destruction, until finally, there was nothing left but rubble and bones.

As he found his strength again, he walked toward the city gates, the stench of sulfur and burnt flesh making him retch. Corpses lined the streets. Feeble, rasping breaths came from those still in agony, and a putrid yellow smoke rose from the ground. But Idbash could not see and could not hear. He stumbled blindly through the ruins until he reached the plains again. Here, the smoke cleared, and he could once more behold the blue sky.

Looking around, searching for something, for someone, his gaze fell upon the mountains. Standing high above him, looking down unto the destruction, were Abraham's tribe. Their armor and spears glinted in the sun, but their eyes were cold as ice. Behind them, on the other side of the mountains, where the city of Gomorrah had once stood, a column of foul smoke rose toward the sky. And Idbash knew.

Slowly, deliberately, he turned once more toward Sodom. Without glancing back, he walked into the city.

IN THE DISTANCE, A CLAP OF THUNDER

David Anderson

The rock smashed against Rodger's face with a sickening smack as the mob continued to hurl stones at him, and the *Chenku* Class Vessel Captain lurched forward, almost passing out from pain as a dirt clod burst on his back, obviously being mistaken for a rock by one of the villagers. A soldier of Gomorrah stepped forward, picking the captain up by the arm and dragging him away to the quarters of the head city guard. The implant in Rodger's inner ear automatically translated any speech to English, allowing him to understand the words of his captors.

"From what province or land do you come, stranger?" said a large tan man in a robe and armored sandals. He aimed the point of a sword at Rodger's head, indicating that he wanted a response. Unfortunately, the translator didn't work both ways, and he didn't know how to talk back to them, a problem that was usually avoided by not talking to the locals on these types of expeditions. It was always observance-only on these safaris, as mandated by legislation back home. Nothing that could potentially alter the timeline was allowed.

"Perhaps you wish to suffer the same fate as your friend?" the head guard asked as he repeated his inquiries. Rodger wanted to answer, but he couldn't. He spoke in English to the man, but it only confused matters.

Rodger was taken to a small arena. Very small compared to the likes of what Rome would build one day, but large enough for a hundred or so fans and onlookers to gather, with ample space for an armored fight to the death. Rodger had the impression, from what he knew of history, that he wouldn't get any of said armor. But his executioners surely would.

Before he was ushered into the fighting area, he saw Cable Paternhorrn's body being dragged away, the right side smashed in and beyond all recognition. Rodger had seen his left side, which was intact enough to identify the man.

Paternhorrn had been a famous architect back home and could afford, like any trillionaire, to entertain himself by travelling backward in time. Most hunted big game, like dinosaurs, or took boats out hunting for a Megalodon or two. But Paternhorrn had been a man who loved history, and he had wanted to witness the destruction of Sodom and Gomorrah. Rodger hated the man for wanting to go back in time for such a dangerous quest, or to be more specific, a situation too dangerous for the entire crew.

Time travel was done via a United States *Chenku* Class Armada Cruiser, a space carrier designed for both Earth and orbital military domination. Space, air, and ground superiority. Ultimately, these ships were equipped for temporal manipulation, the idea being to travel back in time before a catastrophic attack and stop it. With this technology, the United States dominated all other countries, and eventually the U.N. established the entire world as a Pro-American territory. War was effectively ended. The Military-Industrial Complex, still needing to generate some kind of revenue in a world with no war, turned towards the leisure industry, specifically for the extremely wealthy.

Travel to planets within the solar system, deep space exploration, and even time travel became pastimes the super-rich could enjoy. Paternhorrn had a thing for witnessing disasters and had already traveled to 2001 to witness the World Trade Center attacks. And the trade center attack of 2020.

Something else was wrong. Two soldiers had Paternhorrn's backpack and were pulling various packaged food items, LCD maps, high-powered telescopes, and surveillance equipment out of it. They handed some to a man in a wagon, who was apparently traveling to the neighboring town for trade. The situation had passed the point of containment. Dragon Protocol had to be initiated.

"Guess you won't be doing much talking, then," said the soldier who escorted Rodger into the arena fighting area and closed an iron gate behind him.

Rodger was handed a paltry wooden sword that was but a child's toy, and soon, men in metal and leather armor with real weapons arrived, causing the crowd to cheer. A man with a trident stepped forward, his body language indicating he was readying for a stabbing motion but was vaporized when a blinding light struck the arena with tremendous force.

"Captain Smith, Rodger, can you hear me?" said Erinkee Valdez, his female second-in-command.

"This is Captain Rodger Smith. I hear you, Ms. Valdez," Rodger said as he watched the smoke and dust clear.

"We used the precision mining laser as a weapon, sir, disabling the man who was about to attack you. Seems we reestablished contact just in time," she said, telling Rodger that the U.S.S. Gideon was okay and had only been temporarily disabled by solar radiation. It was bad timing, given that Paternhorrn had been captured during that time, along with Rodger himself.

"Thanks, but I've got bad news. Paternhorrn lost his pack, and some of his equipment is already on its way out of the city via a spice and goods trader," the captain said with a twinge of pain in his voice. "It's out of our control now. We can't clean this up. At least, not the easy way. I'm ordering Dragon Protocol."

Dragon Protocol was to be initiated when possible un-doable damage to the timeline was going to be done and must be stopped at all costs. This is not limited to but includes leaking of high-tech equipment to indigenous peoples of the past, via U.N. temporal legislation. Incendiary Sulfur Rockets, made up of 30 mini-rockets per missile tube, are used to 'clear out an area with extreme prejudice'. Given the leak of tech here, he had to order it immediately.

Rodger watched as rockets streaming down from the sky, appearing as falling stars among the sky whose sun only freshly set. Sulfurous gas streamed from the individual rockets and lighted on fire the very oxygen of the air itself, creating malevolent fire balls that erupted in great columns from the sky to the ground.

The rockets burnt so hot that sand melted immediately into churning pools of smooth, amber lava, often filling the incendiary craters left behind by the falling rocket shells. Citizens ran as the landscape turned into a hellscape. Rivers of smooth lava formed from sand, carrying them to their ashy deaths.

Rockets hit buildings, melting the roofs, and pouring down thermite-hot debris on Gomorrahn citizens seeking refuge. Half burning sulfur gas consumed the landscape, now a giant pit of steaming lava.

The rockets stopped, and the blasted desert surface glowed red in the falling night. The crew of the Gideon waited until the morning before disembarking, then they returned to their time but reflected on the fact that they had destroyed Gomorrah. They, in fact, caused themselves to come to that moment in time.

As the ship left orbit with a perplexed crew, dawn broke on Gomorrah and a cold wind whipped across the now cooling blast area. Pillars of hardened ash broke under the push of the wind, falling and turning back into a particle form of dust and blowing away.

A solitary bird soared in the sky above the once great city as a caravan from a far-off land, coming to trade, reached the charred borders of Gomorrah.

A man leading the group disembarked his camel, approaching a solitary feather, sitting pristine amongst the cooled ashes. He concluded angels from God had destroyed the city and sent back word to his scribes to record the event.

Dismayed for having traveled a long way but happy to have averted the cruel hand of God, the caravan left for home with no new spices. They had a story to tell instead.

GARBAGE

Guy & Tonya De Marco

Mr. Gray uploaded a new orbital script into the E-DEN's main navigation computer and the forward retros fired in a complex pattern of bursts to place the ship into a stable orbit.

"Tell me again why we're not just dumping our cargo into the local star's corona," said Mr. Silver. "It's just sulfur, and it's worthless on any planetary system."

Mr. Gray turned his one electronic eye to his mechanical friend. "We've been paired for most of our mean time between failure lifetimes. Have I ever let you down before?"

"Yes. There was that time on Vega-2, where you posed as a pimp and tried to rent me as a pleasure-bot."

"Besides that!" said Mr. Gray as he unlocked his wheels and rolled over to the projection table. "You never let anything go. Almost like we're married." He fiddled with the knobs on the table for a few minutes.

Mr. Silver looked out of the forward window. "What planet are we orbiting?"

"Remember that backwater little planet we tried to populate with cattle, and they accidentally became sentient?" Mr. Gray finally hit the correct sequence to light up the projection table and a digital representation of a planet revolved into view.

"Sol-3? That was a dead planet. Who would buy sulfur there?"

Mr. Gray made a staccato chirp that passed for laughter in the robotic culture. "Those cattle escaped that little garden we made, and they've actually expanded to cover large regions of land." He tweaked the knobs again and focused on a couple of cities below their current location.

"I thought they fried when we took off! I hope the authorities don't find them and force them to say where they came from." Mr. Silver shivered, which involved moving his wheels back and forth three centimeters in rapid succession.

"Relax, my fellow in crime. These humanoids have a short life span, so the originals have been dead for thousands of their local years."

Mr. Silver rolled up to the projection table. "So, what are we up to? Are we going to tell them it's unrefined gold?"

"The meatbags are not that stupid. They haven't evolved to a real political system yet, so they still have some mental acuity." Mr. Gray flipped a mental switch and ejected one of the garbage tubes packed with powdered sulfur. "Watch this!"

The projection table showed a red arc from the bottom of their ship to one of the cities on the map. A small blip rode the arc almost all the way down before it disappeared.

"Wait," said Mr. Silver. "Where did it go?"

Mr. Gray chirped again. "The pod burned up. All that's left is a ball of flaming sulfur, which the scanners can't track." He focused the image on the projection table to show where the blob of fire had landed. A large public square now resembled an ant hill with gasoline poured on it. The humanoids ran in crazy directions, some of them on fire and trying to extinguish themselves, others trying to put out the fires that burned about the square.

Mr. Silver looked up at his partner. "I've known you for ages, but I never knew you could do something like this."

Mr. Gray was taken aback. "You don't approve?"

"No!" said Mr. Silver. "I should've had the first shot."

They both chirped together and began to dump their whole load of worthless sulfur onto the cities, trying to calculate exactly where to send each load and betting on the outcome.

"I like this planet. We'll have to come back again," said Mr. Silver as the last pod left and hit a large, towering complex.

"I have it saved in the galactic positioning system as a favorite."

They watched the humanoids that survived the bombardment stream out of the ruined cities for a while before they closed the hatches.

"You always bring me to the best vacation spots," said Mr. Silver.

"There's more to come, I'm sure," said Mr. Gray as he calculated the next jump point and uploaded it to the nav computer. "I can't wait to see how far those little cattle humanoids evolve in a few dozen more generations."

[Untranslatable]

E.S. Wynn

Transcript SM-15746:

The only warning I received came in the form of the flash when [*The Weapon*] hit the center of Sodom. A handful of seconds. Five, maybe.

I am grateful for it.

I'm grateful because it was more time than most were given.

[*The Library*] has been my home for almost fifty years, and now I fear it will become my tomb. If you're familiar with Sodom as it was before the sudden strike that erased it from existence, surely you've seen [*The Library*]. It was beautiful once—a spiraling tower of gold-marbled hunchunite capped with a shining dome of polished platinum and perched amongst the trees at the southern edge of the city, just beyond the university district. I–I remember cursing how far I had to walk to get there sometimes, but now . .

Now, I'm starting to think that maybe [*The Library*]'s distance from the city center was the only reason I survived.

Most of [*The Library*] is gone. Fifteen floors. [*The Weapon*]?

[*Untranslatable–*]

How foolish war is. All that knowledge. All those texts—gone, lost, fused and melted, and shattered. Thousands of years of knowledge erased in an instant. All that's left is this basement, these archives, these back-up copies of critical texts.

I never thought that [*The Enemy*] would use [*The Weapon*]. They always threatened our nation with it. War is like that. Threats, espionage, some fighting, little skirmishes, but never . . . never something like this. Never something capable of killing so many so quickly.

So many, so many dead. Even if Sodom is the only city that was attacked—even if Gomorrah or Admah or Zeboim still stand, even if our nation is still strong ....

Millions. Millions called Sodom home. Millions.

[*Untranslatable*]

I don't have long. A few days. The gold and platinum in the ruins are probably keeping my exposure down, but how much radiation is still getting through? The bit of the dome I can see is probably covered with more rubble than I can move, and it's all still too hot to touch. There's nothing to eat down here, nothing to drink. Just me, with my burns, my blisters, and my books.

[*Untranslatable*]

I have decided that this will be my last message. There are others, earlier messages, but. . .

Sodom is gone. There's nothing I can do about that now. There is no one out there who's going to see this, not until long after I'm dead, anyway. No point in making more recordings. For the record, my name is [*Untranslatable*] and I am—I *was* the head archivist of [*The Library*]. I have family in Belai. If our nation still stands, if Belai still stands, send word to my uncle. Tell him of Sodom. Tell him that I love him.

That's—that's all.

[*Untranslatable*]

* * *

SODOM SPEAKS: IS THE BIBLE WRONG?

From Puff-Host News Online | TECH

Every child who has ever gone to Sunday school knows the story of Sodom and Gomorrah, but is the story that we know from the Bible a lie?

In 1977, the remains of a woman were discovered in what archaeologists first described as "an elaborate tomb" packed with shattered crystals. These remains (along with the crystals) were scheduled to be repatriated in Jordan in 1981, but, in a stunning twist of luck, were lost in a shuffle of relics from one museum archive to another. Lost, that is, until Nusrat Akhtiar, an intern at the University of Pennsylvania Museum of Archaeology and Anthropology discovered the mistake in 2005 and began to investigate the relics. Careful analysis of the crystals revealed that they were not formed naturally (as was originally suspected) but rather were artificially grown thousands of years ago in some as-yet unknown process.

"On a hunch," Akhtiar said, "I sent a sample [of one of the crystals] to a friend of mine at Los Alamos. A co-worker of his, Doctor Jorge Rinker, identified the crystals as a form of quartz doped with europium."

[Click Here: A.I. And The Rise of Big Data]

And that's where things get weird. Tests performed on the crystal sample quickly revealed the presence of strange patterns within the quartz itself. These patterns, while faint, turned out to be the visual traces of a form of quantum data storage that was, at that time, still only a theory.

"It was really incredible," Doctor Rinker said. "When we realized these ancient crystals were packed with, literally, terabytes of data, we couldn't stop asking questions. Who made them? Who used them? Why were they there? What could we learn from them if we could only access and translate the data they held?"

And it was only last year that Doctor Rinker and his team were finally able to begin answering some of those questions.

[Click Here: The Quantum Mechanics of Love]

"I remember the first images [Doctor Rinker] sent me," Akhtiar said. "Most of the data within the crystals I sent was holografic (sic). They were having trouble sorting through all the different data channels, but there were pictures sometimes, very clear pictures of people, of buildings."

"We were working closely with a team in Germany and another team in China," Doctor Rinker told us on Tuesday. "The Chinese were the first ones to tie the coding together into a working emulator capable of turning the data on the crystals into two-dimensional images and films. Most of the first crystals we decoded were educational texts on basic math, conjugation, et cetera."

But the crystal fragment known as SM-15746 held something altogether different.

"A message, they told me," Akhtiar said, "left by the woman who had died in that place. She was an archivist. The tomb was not a tomb, but a library. Probably the most important library in the biblical city of Sodom."

[Click here to watch the SM-15746 message over at Penn Museum's Official Website]

While some biblical scholars are calling the recording a hoax, many scientists in the fields of Anthropology, Quantum Computing and Linguistics are coming forward to vouch for the "crystal message" of SM-15746. "This changes everything we know about the past," Doctor Chartrand of Stanford University said during a talk about SM-15746. "The people of Sodom were far more advanced than anyone has ever believed possible. They were more advanced than us, but they were not immune to the stupidity of war."

[Click Here: Ukraine Unrest – Top 20 Pics]

Most of the crystals from the Library of Sodom have yet to be accessed or translated, but as Doctor Rinker said during an interview on CNN, "these crystals hold a lot of promise. We're learning things. Incredible things. I can't wait to see what wonders we'll find in the coming weeks, months, and years."

[Click Here: Will Gay Rights Lead to Human Extinction?]

THE SALT PIT

JD DeHart

When Nephesh moved into the town, he was blown away by the vastness of the metropolis. Compared to the twin cities, his hometown was just a dot in the desert. There was a noticeable scent of brine in the air that never seemed to leave, burning the nostrils.

Perhaps it had addled the brains of the residents. Perhaps that was why they danced late into the night, their tattoos singing and their chains rattling, binding and wrapping each other. Perhaps that was why they had worshipped the beast, resting on its haunches in the middle of the cities, a smile on its face that said, "Welcome, have some fun, do not go away."

The first night in the twin cities, Nephesh made the company of a bright young girl. Everyone else seemed to be giants bathed in ebony, but she was a light, wisp, paper-thin angel.

"Welcome," she said to him in her lovely voice.

"What is all the ruckus about?" Nephesh had asked. Now, he knew.

"That is the way it always is," she said. It was only a few hours later that he saw her, dancing in the middle of the procession, and later he found her corpse, drained dry and broken.

That is the way it always is.

Of course, at first, he told himself that he would be nothing like the people. He was disgusted with the way they lived their lives. Their rituals were disgusting to him. Then, one day, he noticed some bright fruit being offered up at a late-night festival. He did not know the god to whom the sacrifice was offered.

Never mind the flashing gold masks, the dancing calf, and the pools of blood. Never mind the neighbors in the throes of their own interests. He was here only because he had a simple hunger: an empty stomach that wanted a bite of fruit.

As he chewed the rind, he thought again and again of the tiny white angel he had met on his first night. He thought about the endless stream of bodies he had seen, the damage piled up from deranged vigils.

Then, he began to feel lonely and so started attending festivals out of habit, to fill the need to see others, even if their conversation was breathy, intermittent, and staccato.

There was always the possibility of leaving, but something in the fruit—some nectar—made him want to stay. Once he had tasted, he both wanted and did not want to leave at the same time. He knew he could not, because the next town might not have this addictive harvest.

In the darkness of the final night, Nephesh began to dance. He swayed to the animal music and began to taste more than ever. His fingers ran over streams of blood, and he turned around in the middle of the ceremony, facing the beast, only to find he had become the beast. He backed away from the image of himself, the claws and the fragments of skin dangling from his lips.

Something inside—a voice, a conscience—said, *there is still hope*, but the physiognomy of the beast was glittering. There was promise in its panther stride, even if the promise did not deliver.

Then the air became thicker, the salt condensing, and a great heat moved through the masses.

They did not even pause in their celebration. Tiny forms swept away in the blast, the occasional figure made permanent in a statue of salinity.

PAYMENT

Gary Hewitt

Two guards approached.

"Why are you here?"

"I have come to see if the stories are true."

Two lowered rifles met the visitor's chest.

"What have you heard?"

"The rich prosper, and the poor are fucked."

The elder of the sentries snorted and kept his gun level.

"Are you rich or target practice?"

"Check your records and look for Mr. Kitchener."

He made a call and put his weapon away.

"Go straight to Big Eddie. It's up the end of the street."

The great steel gateway yawned apart. Mr Kitchener straightened his Porkpie hat and handed the sentry a hundred-dollar bill. He received a "no thanks."

The street was immaculate with several neon towers on each side of the road. Promises of sex, addiction, and wealth screamed for attention. His gaze lingered upon a sign promising tastes of the forbidden upon the forsaken. Another promised the weak a way to be dominated and taken.

Images assaulted his vision of screaming naked men and women chained upon steel altars under the gaze of suited men and women.

Big Eddie's mansion dwarfed the other buildings. Granite-muscled women armed with crossbows ushered him to an escalator. Several seconds later he crossed a quartz floor to greet a half-naked man being fed strawberries and peaches by a tiny doll-girl.

"Mr Kitchener, you will just love it here."

"I have never seen such depravity."

"You'll be staying at Kitten Plaza. I've already assigned you several broads to entertain you."

Mr Kitchener slammed his briefcase upon the desk.

"What's this?"

"My deposit."

Eddie grinned and pressed the brass buttons. The case opened to reveal a curious black box with one flashing red light.

"What the fuck is this?"

"You're being shut down."

Eddie reached into his drawer. A revolver pointed straight at the center of Kitchener's head.

"I'll shut you down. I'll ask you again, what the hell is this damn box?"

"A signal."

Hell awoke outside. Explosions and flames rained down. Towers tumbled into oblivion. Eddie screamed when he burst into a human cauldron of fat and flames.

Kitchener ignored the planes as they flew past and readied for another pass. He took the stairs, oblivious to the fatal heat and smoke. His clothes remained unmolested and not a bead of angelic sweat trailed from his brow. He opened his mobile.

"Yeah, it's me. Just to let you know, Sodom is sorted. I'll take care of Gomorrah tomorrow."

THICK AIR

Terry Alexander

The thick sulfur dust hung in the air like a hot mist. The slave master moaned at my feet. A flaming yellow ball struck his leg and reduced it to ash. I slipped the rope from my neck as he screamed in agony.

"James, help me. Save me and win your freedom." Pain etched deep lines across his face. "Save me."

My shaking hands closed on his robes and tore a long strip of cloth free. I tied it across my face to filter the thick air. His weak hands pawed at my legs. Blinking away the tears, I stared down at the man who had tormented me for nearly a year.

"Please, James, save me." His face blistered from the hot powder falling from the sky. "Save me." His hands fastened on the hem of my slave tunic. He was trying to pull me down.

I kicked him in the face. The blisters popped, draining a thick clear liquid. The sole on my sandal tore through his cheek. Blood gushed from the split flesh as panic gripped my heart. I gazed around, looking for the authorities. Rebellious slaves are dealt with quickly, savagely, by dismemberment and death.

A woman, her garments blazing, ran down the wide avenue. A hot yellow ball stuck to her middle, burning through cloth and tender flesh. She stepped on my master's face, leaving a huge gob of flaming sandal on his cheek. His agonized screams intensified. The woman tripped and fell. She clawed at the gooey substance. Her hands burst into flames. She disappeared in the swirling yellow mist. Her screams mixed with a hundred others, building to an inhuman, ear-piercing shriek.

The flaming balls splattered on the hard surfaces, sticking to whatever they hit and burning uncontrollably. The slanted roof of Sarah's Palace jutted from the gloom, a place known for its debauchery. It might have been my salvation. The yellow rain died away. Leaping the flaming obstacles, I managed to make it to the palace with only minor burns.

My heart thumped wildly in my chest as I pressed my back against the wall, grateful for the protection and the opportunity to catch my breath. In the street, men, women, and children ran back and forth like chickens. Every instinct I had screamed at the impossibility of what had occurred. This flaming rain can't be happening. Bodies covered the street: rich and poor, slave and master, whore and whoremonger, each one incinerated by an impossible fire that burned through the stone structures of Sodom.

A large ball of sulfur struck the mansion and shook it down to the foundation. Walls buckled, and portions of the roof slid away. The wall grew hot against my back. My tunic smoldered. The slave whores burst from the collapsing building, filling the street, their naked bodies covered with hot sulfuric grit. Several blundered into a pool of burning goo. Smoke rose from bare feet and burst into flames. The stronger women shoved the weaker to the ground and used their bodies as a fleshy bridge to safety.

I pushed myself away from the palace. Ignoring the pain along my shoulder blades, I ran down the street. The outside wall must be close. I had to clear the wall and make my way to the woodlands to survive.

Pitiful moans filled my ears. Blobs of cooked flesh moved and twitched beneath my feet. They didn't resemble people any longer. Fingerless hands slapped my legs. Mumbled pleas filled my ears with promises of sex and great wealth. I ignored them all. I had to reach the wall and find a way over before the fury of the storm resumed.

I made my way down the street, walking across the bodies of the dead and dying. I recognized a face. Mary looked at me with pleading eyes. Her injuries were too severe; I looked the other way and kept moving. Heat transferred from their seared flesh through the soles on my sandals into my feet. Air and gas burst from the bodies each time my foot settled on a chest or stomach.

"Slave," a harsh female voice shouted. "Come here. I command you."

Sarah, the owner of the slave whores, stood in the mansion's entryway, her white garments torn and dotted with burn spots. I cleansed years of slave training from my mind and remembered the beating I received for real or imagined mistakes. I ignored the woman and kept walking, more determined than ever to make my way out of the city and survive.

"Slave!" Her speed was unbelievable, a hand closed on my shoulder. "I should kill you for your disobedience." She held a silver dagger in her hand. The tip pricked my neck. "Get me to safety and I'll spare your life."

"We must make haste." I glanced at the dark clouds swirling overhead and knew the firestorm was returning with new fury. "Step on the bodies. We must get over the wall and into the forest."

"Put this around your neck." She pulled a braided golden rope from her robe and tossed one end to me. "You belong to me now. If you try to escape, I'll kill you."

I stared at the rope for an instant. Then I met her eyes.

"Put it on." She jabbed the sharp tip into my flesh. Blood welled from the wound and crept down my throat.

I slipped the rope over my head and moved forward. Sarah was more squeamish than I realized. The scent of charred flesh seemed to upset her. I'd seen her slice the nose and eyelids from a female slave the previous year without batting an eye. She hesitated at each footfall, placing each foot gingerly on the cooked flesh. We moved forward in a jerky motion. The rope tightened around my throat several times, choking me.

A stomach ruptured under Sarah's sandal. Her foot sank into the intestines and offal. She fell to her knees. Hot bile burst from her throat. The scent of roasted dung poisoned the air. Tears filled her eyes. The moisture collected the yellow dust swirling in the breeze. She tried to rise. The rib bones held her foot tightly. The hem of her garment dipped into a gooey deposit of sulfur, and the robe burned like a candle wick. She slapped at the blaze, transferring the sticky substance to her hands.

"Slave! Slave!" Her panicked screams rose to a crescendo. "Save me, slave."

I yanked the rope from her hand and jumped to the nearest body, away from her short arm and sharp dagger. "Nay, woman. Find your own way out."

"Damn you," she cursed. "Damn you for a coward."

"I hope to be a living coward." I placed my foot gingerly on the body of a dead whore. A burning pain shot through my back. I pitched forward to my knees. Feeling for the source of my pain, my hand closed around the dagger hilt. I glanced back at Sarah.

She managed a lop-sided smirk even as the inferno consumed her body. "My life is far more precious than yours. You're nothing but a slave, unfit to survive."

I pulled the blade free and tossed it to the ground. Hot, sticky blood gushed from the wound. Bits of sulfur dust pelted my skin, carried on the swirling winds. The thick air returned, I gasped for air, and my lungs burned. Thunder rumbled above my head. A flaming ball of sulfur struck the street and splattered like an obese rain drop.

I stumbled forward. My tear-filled eyes focused on the outside wall. A group of blind men, their clothes burned away, bodies covered with large, puckered wounds, clogged the street. I fought through them to the stairs. A sizzling blob struck the stone near my hand. Bits of goo burned through my skin. I forced my legs to move, slowly, one painful step at a time. I reached the top and gazed out at the woodland beyond. The sulfur rain grew with intensity. The forest was in flames. All was lost. I sat on the wall and waited for the end.

ZACHARIAH

Melchior Zimmermann

Zachariah ran up the hill, his feet flying over the yellow brimstone. Here and there, billows of smoke escaped from between the smoldering rocks. From time to time, he could glimpse a piece of charred limestone, remnants of a house or palace.

Zachariah's father had told him that before the great destruction there had been a mighty city in this place. His ancestors had lived here, prospering through their prowess in trade and craftsmanship. But five years ago, when Zachariah had only been two years old, the hill tribes had declared war on them. They had beseeched their powerful god to help them in their battle, and he had rained fire and brimstone upon the mighty city of Gomorrah. Unable to ward off the wrath of the heathen god, his ancestors had fled the city. Few of them had made it alive.

As they were roaming through the plains in search of a new home, the hill tribes had descended upon them, killing man, woman, and child, and slicing the throats of their livestock. Only a few dozen managed to escape this second onslaught. Alone, left with nowhere to go, his family decided to head back to Gomorrah to rebuild their home.

Now, five years later, all there was left was a lonesome encampment near the smoldering ruins of the once-famous city. The people there managed to survive through trade, exchanging the pure sulfur from their home for crops and meat. Nothing would grow on the scorched earth, and if they tried to settle new lands, the hill tribe would massacre them on sight.

Zachariah looked down upon the wasteland that surrounded him. In the far-off distance, he could see the sun glinting off the endless sea. To the south lay the hills of his enemies, and to the north, their sister-city Sodom, who had suffered the same fate. They were the only people who would trade with Gomorrah in good faith, and the only ones who respected their traditions and customs.

The adults, Zachariah had come to realize, were resigned to their fate. Instead of trying to better their lives, they simply did their best to survive. There was no hope left in their eyes, and no spring in their steps. But it was not so for him.

Zachariah had decided that he would rebuild the city of his fathers. He would keep alive their traditions and work tirelessly until tales of their glory once again rang through the land. And once his people had regained their rightful place, he would remember the hill tribe, and their god.

SINGLE RIGHTEOUS SEEKS SAME

Lyda Morehouse

Sodom was not the place to try to find love and redemption. I should've known that, yet I came to this den of iniquity seeking those very things. Now I'd die for my troubles.

Fire rained from the ceiling.

The Rover's missiles had some kind of acid in them. The space station melted around me. Tiny, pinprick-size holes dripped a toxic, foul-smelling rain. The air stunk of sewage and something akin to a spent match.

Groups of people—most of them tourists in their smart military uniforms and fancy dresses—clustered together clogging the once glittering Broadway of the space station. Some raged, some sobbed, some screamed hysterically. Others stared blankly at nothing at all, already part of the living dead. There were a few fools like me, desperately searching faces, trying to find that one person among hundreds of thousands.

Sodom and Gomorrah had been built to outsource Earth's sins and sinners, on two spinning, orbiting space stations full of lust and lasciviousness. The Hegemony couldn't fight a religious war against the Rovers if they didn't have God on their side, could they? Better to ship sin off world.

I'd spent fifteen thousand credits to buy my 'indulgence' to Sodom. I didn't even know if Angel was really here. It was where she would go; it was where they all went—those branded with the Mark of Cain.

Another boom shook the station. No, that was inaccurate—a trick of my mind trying to make sense of the strangeness of space battle: the sound was actually more of a 'suck.' The vacuum of space collapsed something nearby, crumbling it in on itself.

I should have married Angel.

If I'd married Angel, no Hegemony officer could've touched her. Marriage was a sacrament. God trumped everything in the Hegemony. God was a fucking loophole.

Angel and I grew up together, playing Hegemony and Rovers, like all the kids in our multiplex did—screaming up and down the halls evading the old neighbor's dirty looks and his drunken attempts to whip his door open just as we ran past. The old man finally managed to nail our buddy Ayokunle that way. We'd laughed and laughed, despite Ayokunle's twelve stitches and the stern lectures from our parents. After a week of half-hearted penance, we were back at it, Ayokunle trundling along with us, a freshly whitened scar on deep brown skin. We'd all seemed invulnerable then. I was too young to understand what Angel would become.

No, was *always*, even then.

Another grinding sound reverberated through the walls. My feet bounced awkwardly as gravity began to fail, our rotation degrading. Something dripped onto my head. I smelled the choking odor of burning flesh. My flesh.

The first time Angel asked me to marry her I thought it was a joke. She'd been wearing these adorable, retro, tea-length skirts. We were arguing about them because she wanted to wear them all the time and the baseball coach was going to kick her off the team if she didn't wear a proper uniform. She was our best pitcher, but I wasn't lying when I told her that she looked just as cute in the uniform with her long, silky black ponytail sticking out the back of the ball cap. "Lots of girls play baseball," I told her. Hell, hadn't we just played that mixed team from

Holy Oak? All those girls wore a uniform and not one of them was as pretty as my Angel.

"I might be in love with you a little bit," Angel had said, her voice cracking. "Marry me?"

I laughed and said sure, but I didn't mean it. I just didn't want to lose my best friend, or our best pitcher.

The alarms cut off a second before the lights failed. Screams rose to replace claxons. We were plunged into total darkness. Emergency lights flickered valiantly, albeit weakly, revealing the corridor in a dim haze. My heart hammered in my chest and my huffing breath made ice crystals in the freezing air.

It felt close now, the end.

Everyone in the multiplex looked after Angel as best we could. Her parents loved their only daughter and so they did everything to make Angel's life easier. *Everything.* Her voice evened out, stopped cracking, just as mine settled deeper. She went away for a couple of months that last summer, 'to emersion camp,' everyone joked, but when she came back not one boy could keep their eyes off her, nor half the girls either. She was always stunning but going away had made her beautiful.

If no one had reported her, that would have been the end of it.

I could tell, when they came to brand and deport her, Angel thought I had betrayed her. It wasn't. I should have said 'yes' when she asked me to marry her, but I swear that was my only sin against her.

Everyone had tried to stop them, but they tazed us, beat us, and dragged her away from us. The only comfort was that I never heard her screams. I never had to see that horrible letter burned into her, searing her soul with its foul accusations. I was with Ayokunle, in jail, serving my time for assaulting an officer and obstructing justice. Like half the multiplex. We hadn't let Angel go without a fight. I was proud of that, at least.

On Sodom, branding marks were everywhere. Scarlet letters, some people called them. I never understood what half of them meant. I was told that Angel's face would be scarred with a "T." When I asked the

Tour Guide what that stood for, he'd sneered and said, "Trap, son. T stands for Trap. You got to watch out for those. You think you're buying one thing, but you get a whole other."

I threw up on the Tour Guide's shoes.

I was nineteen. I didn't know myself. I thought that being with her said something about me.

And now, too late, I knew it *did*—it said I was selfish and a fool.

I saw her then. A second before the blinding flash rent the station asunder, our eyes met. My apology froze in the vacuum of space.

IOTA

SODOM

Meg Eden

When the sky grew dark
and yellow, someone laughed:
It's the end of the world!

Well, fuck! I said
and let in
my next customer.

Men and women
knock down my doors
to have sex with me,

I charge them now
to avoid
an affront to my body.

Sometimes
my customers
are animals—

I do not like it with animals
but it causes a sensation
and pays well.

The customer who came
when the air went bad
asked if it was my scent,

so I closed the window
and said the streets
expire from bad people.

He laughed,
but inside of me
there was an earthquake.

The god
I acknowledge
is the god of my body,

who has brought me
out from
the land of slavery.

The light in the room
went red, and
outside there was a great

shout, and the sound
of hail, pelting
the walls like a missionary.

The man cried
and reached
for my breasts,

but I turned from him
and opened
the window:

the sky
was a great flame

and we were all embers.

A heavy smoke cloud
came over us
so that the homes

were hidden, and all
that was left
were silent ashes.

I coughed
and could not stop
coughing.

Closing the window,
the sulfur stung my eyes
so that I could not see,

and the man wept:
Why, God?
lowering onto my bed.

We were on the city wall
and there was no
sanctuary for us.

As my throat
burned its own fire,
the sky collapsed

and the man's skin
lit up. He ran
across the room—

his own self-
contained sun—
but found no peace.

And I remained

until the fire
found me here,

and the hand of a mourning
just God
could not bear me.

I do not repent.

SHORT STORIES

RUINS OF GOMORRAH

Nicholas Paschall

I open my eyes slowly, ignoring the muck that has half submerged my body in the sinking mire that was once our great city. I claw my way free, ignoring the torn scraps of skin peeling off my body as I scrabble up the foundation of an old tavern I used to frequent; now I live in the rubble like some utter street trash.

That's what we are now: street trash and monsters.

Stooped low behind a section of wall, I shuffle to a table that I've set up as a small shrine, muttering a small prayer as my day begins. Perhaps I'll find food today?

I hear a scream in the distance, as well as the crumbling of another building. *That sounds promising,* I think.

Turning, I scoop up the sword I'd scavenged and lope onto the street, avoiding the craters of still-broiling sulfur that made this city an inferno. I jog around the impact craters, past others like me as they awaken to the sounds of the screams. If I move fast enough, I'll be the first to get there.

Nobody comes to our fair city anymore. Well, nobody sane, that is. Heretics and worshippers of the devil flock here, seeing it as a holy site for their profane rituals and horrid rites. I still have faith—I have faith that God will save us. He will let us leave the still-burning ruins of our city. For some reason, any and all who called Gomorrah home can't leave this place. We start to choke and suffocate as the cool air of the open plains meets us. It's as if we've become accustomed to the darkness that now envelops this land, and we are cursed by God for its sins.

I leap over a small crater, knocking up some loose stone as I land. I bleat in pain as one of the rocks causes me to twist my ankle, but I pay it no mind: I smell fresh food amongst the steamy haze of sulfur and brimstone.

Squatting in the road, behind the upper portion of a clay roof that was blasted into the street, I see them: A wagon being pulled by two oxen, with an older man in the bullock seat and four young men walking beside it. A woman sits next to the older man, cradling a young child against her chest. That makes my mouth water at the very thought. Fresh child! How long had it been since I had a child to slake my hunger upon?

"I don't know, Ezekiel," one of the men on foot says, looking up at the driver of the cart. "This doesn't seem right. This is supposed to be Gomorrah, but nobody's here!"

"Yeah, and what's with these craters?" Another man carrying a sword asks. "They have burning pitch in them, or something. How are we supposed to do trade with a city with nobody in it?"

"I don't know," Ezekiel says, pulling on the reins to make the oxen stop. He rubs his wrinkled brow, wiping away the sweat forming on his face. "This isn't right, not at all. The man said that this would be a good place to sell our wares."

Man? I rise to have a better look at the group through the haze. *What man? Who would send them to this godforsaken pile of rubble when there's barely enough left to go around as it is?*

"What's that over there?" One of the men calls out, pointing in my direction. The haze of sulfuric clouds makes it difficult for anyone not used to them to see. "Hello? Can you help us?"

I clear my throat, coughing a bit to get my voice back. "I can be of some assistance. It's just too hard to reach you. Come closer, leave your cart, and skirt around the crater so I can give you directions."

I can see in my peripheral vision several other survivors such as myself moving through the steaming clouds, their hooves clacking softly on the stone as they move to flank the group. One lets out a soft bleating noise as he crosses some busted wooden boards, causing the men to look for its origin.

"I'm a shepherd looking for his flock," I say as I move around a vent of sulfurous smoke roiling from a small crater. "I was in the countryside, and my sheep ran into the city for some reason."

"We can help you find them," one of the men says, squinting into the thick mist. A man to his right coughs, nearly retching at the scent of the air around him. I breathe deeply and smile.

"Where are you?" A third man calls out as they maneuver around the crater. Already, I can see that Ezekiel has five of my brethren swarming his cart, muffling his screams with blades. The oxen will taste mighty fine after we've made a proper sacrifice of them.

I walk out of the column of broiling sulfur, my fur ruffling as I step over the vent. I rear my head back and bleat loudly, earning a number of responsive bleats from all around. The men stare at me unabashedly, giving me a chance to lower my head and charge at them, blade held in both hands, low and dragging along the ground.

I ram one man in the side with my head, my curved horns and thick skull allowing me to break him in a single blow. He flies off me with a scream, hitting a crumbling pylon with a spine-snapping howl. His friends look on in amazement as I slash up, spearing my sword into the first man hard enough to lift him off the ground. Hacking up blood, the grip on his sword goes limp enough for me to wrestle it away from him, and I push him to the side as I now face his last two friends.

"What in God's name? Demon!" The fourth man yells, earning a chorus of bleating laughter from my brothers and sisters of the fallen city.

Pulling my lip back in a snarl, I stomp forward, my hooves crushing stone beneath my weight as I move. My belt of skulls clatters ominously as I approach them, the small human sword in my hand ill-suited for my needs as a warrior.

"I am no demon, just a man cursed by God for his sins. Soon he will forgive us of our transgressions, and we'll all be able to leave this cursed land. But not today."

Ezekiel lets out a wounded yelp, causing the two men to turn for a split second as if they can see the fat old man in the distance being eaten or the woman and child being dragged off for stock as slaves. I lunge forward, stabbing the only man who hasn't said anything in the side of the neck, ripping outward in a ham-fisted tug that leaves him bleeding in a wide spray of arterial delight. I laugh.

"Why? What have we done to deserve this?" The last man asks, turning to regard me, gripping his sword in a defensive position.

I give him a look that I doubt he could recognize as loathing. "You come here, full of the glory of Yahweh, and you ask what you've done wrong? Gomorrah is a city best left alone, friend, for those that live there are wicked in their ways. Isn't that what you've been told, hmm?"

The man falters. "Yes. I mean, of course, everyone has heard of Gomorrah's, and Sodom's, rather wild parties."

"We sinned. We sinned so badly that we were punished for it with raining sulfur and brimstone. Those of us who survived were transformed into half-man, half-beast. We are the servants of the devil now, sin incarnate, and of the living flesh. You've made a poor choice in coming here."

He doesn't respond. A small boy, his horns barely even nubs at his temples and his fur short and soft, runs a pike through the man's tunic, spearing him in the back. The man's blood turns his tunic to a dark red. The young one is breathing heavily, and I can tell that this is his first kill.

Good for him.

I grab the front of the bleeding man's tunic and yank him off the pike, pulling him off his feet and close to my muzzle. "We will one day again walk in the light of God … but we will keep any and all who come here from ever leaving, as it is His will."

And with that, I end the young man's life by clamping my jaws over his throat, my blunt teeth grinding away at tissue and veins. I yank back a mouthful of succulent meat, which I savor as I watch the young man struggle to breathe without a throat. I drop him unceremoniously to the ground for the young one, who pounces on him. Turning, I toss the small pig sticker aside and retrieve my blade from the coughing man impaled with it.

Huh … surprised he's still alive. I clop to the man's side, tail swishing lightly behind me.

The man looks at me, a rivulet of blood dribbling past his cracked lips to his chin. "M-m-monster! Th-There is n-no place in h-h-heaven for a beast like you!"

Reaching to grab him by the shoulder with one padded hand and the hilt of my sword with the other, I stare heartily into his eyes.

"We'll see, in the end." I say, yanking my blade free, causing a torrent of blood and bile to spill onto the street. His eyes grow dim, staring back in defiance. His spirit departs before his features soften. "We'll see …"

I begin my meal, eating what I can before my smaller brethren move in for a share of the kill. I fold my hands at my chest as I tear at the meat and say a small prayer, thanking the Lord for this bounty.

Then I dine.

THE MORTICIAN OF SODOM

C.J. Beacham

"See you on the other side," Teodor said. "And remember to breathe."

I grimaced and sat down to catch my breath. After the explosions this morning, I never expected to see another side of anywhere.

#

I woke this morning when the mountain groaned. It had rumbled twice in recent memory, but no stories from the past eight generations mentioned eruption. When the ground shook today, however, windows rattled until one smashed. My eyes popped open. I rose from the lambskin, peered through the crack between the door and frame. Other eyes peered from doorways across the dusty road. Distant explosions and shrill voices echoed from the mountains, and I sensed the odd glow growing towards the cities of the plain.

Over the past two months, old-timers warned the miners not to set fire to the mountains, but thirst for sulfur overpowered their pleas. The sulfur industry bolstered Sodomite commerce, which was dominated by black gunpowder, Sodom's chief export. Generations had made their livings mining sulfur until Kedorlaomer conquered Sodom and exploded the large pits, killing most of the miners inside. After

Kedorlaomer's defeat following the Battle of the Vale, the sons and grandsons of miners gathered gear and headed off to the mountains. After fifteen years of inactivity, the shafts had caved in, their entrances buried under rock-slide debris. During those years, the old-time miners who survived the blast refused to apprentice the next generation. This new generation was cutting-edge, accustomed to gadgets of Sodom's advancing technology, but lacking gritty mineshaft experience. They concocted special instruments to extract the sulfur but couldn't figure out how to blast through the mountain to get to it.

Smoke billowed south from the mountain's direction. I wondered if the top had blown. Over the next few minutes, boulders could be heard rolling down and tumbling off cliffs, even from four miles away. A thick grey cloud plowed southward, low through the sky, and blocked the sun trying to announce the day. The cloud's jagged edges glowed like mustard yellow sheen on a dirty plate. It made me nauseous, and I vomited in the pale under the window.

The next few days would be busy for me, as many dead miners would need to be embalmed and buried.

"Sodom is a fine place for a mortician," my father, Luka, said from his deathbed before he signed the mortuary over to me. He died later that night, his body the first embalmed under my ownership. That was twenty years ago, and thousands of bodies have passed through the mortuary since. But Luka never realized the irony of his claim, nor could he fathom the events of the day awaiting me. Or so I thought.

People were tickled by Kedorlaomer's defeat, but captives freed from his stockades poured into Sodom as well as neighboring Gomorrah and Zeboyim. The freed captives erected strange stalls and ramshackle dwellings in abandoned lots at the corner of Fifth and Sixth. By day they slept, or at least remained out-of-sight. Throughout the night, they danced around to strange music and performed heinous acts under the guise of theatre, all while selling a variety of trinkets, potions, and other useless wares. All manner of phantasm and lewd activity could be witnessed in the camp, and soon residents of Sodom became intrigued. Shop owners, miners, and paupers, even Mayor Bera and Sheriff Hammu found themselves enchanted by The Captives.

Every evening at seven sharp, they kicked off the nightly festivities to honor their leader Teodor, a renowned Fire Starter, though he never showed his face. They summoned flame from thin air, contorted in unnatural ways, and swung from arched contraptions, all while showing body parts Sodomites were unaccustomed to viewing in public. The carnival continued throughout the night, and only when the sun peeked over the horizon did the hedonism wane.

Before The Captives arrived, Sodom was a friendly place, the kind where neighbors sit on porches and respect each other's kids. But The Captives showed Sodom the world beyond the walls. Trash piled up on the street, robberies and sexual crimes increased, and residents no longer welcomed each other into their homes. Poor people were scoffed at and banned from buying food in the markets and left to starve in the streets. Any visitors to Sodom were automatically viewed through squinted eyes, which I found ironic since strangers initiated the change in the first place.

I dressed and scarfed down breakfast then headed for the mortuary. The first bodies would arrive around noon, I figured, and preparations would take until at least then. I took the shortcut across Sixth. As Fifth approached, an unexpected sight crossed my eyes. The Captives were dancing around outside, singing, and playing music with their strange instruments. I'd never seen one of them in the sunlight until at least five o'clock in the afternoon. But on this day, they pranced around as if last night's carnival never stopped.

One dressed as a clown approached me, removed his extra tall hat, and handed me a flier with the simple phrase: *The hour is at hand*. He placed the hat back on his head and bowed with a sinister smile spread across his face. I wadded the paper and tossed it into a pile of balled-up fliers beside his oversized shoes. He laughed through his painted white face.

Another clown approached to apologize, but when I extended my hand to meet his, he squeezed the rose decorating his lapel and squirted water in my eye. This time they both laughed, and tears spilled from their painted black eyes. I never understood why the miners listened to those strangers.

The Captives were masters of fire and heard about the novice miners' dilemma. They sent Teodor, the mysterious leader, to inspect the mountain. He returned to Sodom offering a solution: small pockets of sulfur could be ignited through cracks at the top of the mountain. Once the pockets caught fire, the sulfur would liquefy and run down the side, thereby igniting other pockets as the flow rushed towards the base. The sulfur would pile up, cool down and harden, and be easily extracted at the bottom.

The idea sounded legitimate to the miners. But there was one catch Teodor pointed out—the fire must not burn above 444 degrees, as the sulfur would bypass the liquid stage and go straight to gas.

Even greenhorn miners knew that gaseous sulfur is lethal. Here was the angle: in return for a twenty percent share, Teodor would ignite the fires and guarantee the temperature remained below 440 degrees. After two nights of discussion and a final vote, the Miners' Council agreed to Teodor's proposal. He set the first blaze two months ago, and until now, the project proceeded safely. The mines produced more sulfur each day than the previous one, and as exports increased, profits began to flow. Teodor's twenty percent added up quickly.

Last week, a group of miners complained about the slow process and claimed the extraction rate could be increased. Teodor warned that multiple fires would raise temperatures to threatening levels, a natural inferno he would be unable to control. The Council ignored him. Three nights ago, they voted to increase the number of fires set each day. Last night, Teodor headed for the mountain to set multiple fires.

I shook off the clowns like dogs do water and continued towards the mortuary. The fierce cloud now rumbled near Sodom's north gate, emitting plumes of ash that expanded to fill the space around it. Lightning crackled around the edges like ungrounded electrical wires. Though the sun rose, its light and heat were blocked from reaching the ground.

Sodomites emerged onto the streets. Bent necks with wide eyes peered into the sky. They whispered and shrugged their shoulders, wondering what wrath was being cast upon them. I urged them to return indoors before sulfur began falling. Most stared at me with empty eyes, unable to comprehend or refusing to heed the warning.

They stood in the streets dumbfounded, gazing with open mouths at the approaching storm. I hustled to the mortuary and ducked inside just as the first particulates reached the ground. Within minutes, the mustard-yellow mass hovered over the city, and the Sodomites waited underneath it as the first fireball fell. It lit the sky for only a second, but the blue flame revealed the cloud's immense sulfur content.

Teodor arrived at the mountain about midnight to set the fires. He sensed high sulfur concentration in a particular crack and decided to begin there. Whether or not he knew the pocket extended to the other side of the mountain, and upward to the top, remains unknown.

The initial fire burned with ferocity and spread through the pocket at unexpected volume and speed. Even so, Teodor continued lighting fires on other parts of the mountain as instructed by the Council. As dawn approached, the first miners arrived and cheered the blazes. Gold coins flashed before their eyes. But when the sun peeked over the horizon, they realized the fires were burning out of Teodor's control. Some stood by to watch the growing inferno. Others returned to Sodom to deliver the news.

The first returning miners passed by the mortuary as sulfur mist began floating to the ground like scragged cotton balls. They urged Sodomites to take cover inside their dwellings. The yellowy-grey mass planted itself over Sodom, howled like a pack of rabid dogs, and swirled sand and stone with tumultuous crosswinds. Bolts of fire shot between the smaller clouds that conjoined to form the mass.

Panic gripped the Sodomites as the cloud bore down upon the city. Men gathered valuables such as gold coins, family heirlooms, and lambs. Women rounded up the children and elders. In moments, most of Sodom's residents moved *en masse* to the southern wall, attempting to escape as rain increased intensity. Some Sodomites realized it was impossible to outrun the sinister threat. These folks lingered in the streets to accept fate or huddled under overhangs to watch havoc wreaked. The Captives continued the carnival during the day with no audience, unimpeded by the first sulfur drifts and impending carnage. They danced and played and sang as if the entire town of Sodom was crowded into their makeshift theatre cheering on the performance.

The miners who stayed at the mountain gathered with Teodor, who believed he could gain control over the fury. He sat on a flattened boulder and recited incantations, calling for mercy upon the cities of the plain.

The miners, who were accustomed to technological fixes, scorned Teodor for depending on superstition, despite the fact they had no other recourse to stop the blazes. They pointed and laughed as he sang in languages they didn't understand. The mountain hissed and popped and groaned. Soon, sulfur particles drifted through the air and burned sores into their skin on contact.

None of the miners realized they stood at the epicenter, the seething cauldron summoned to destroy the cities of the plain. They did notice, however, how Teodor sat unencumbered, even as the putrid mist enshrouded them. The miners snickered and sneered at him as they gasped for breath, their eyes burning past tears. And still Teodor sat like a statue, breathing slowly, singing his songs. As they lay dying, the miners watched thick ash trail off the mountain toward the plain and coalesce into an ominous mass approaching Sodom.

The mighty cloud castigated Sodom. Those of us inside stone buildings were protected and witnessed the destruction firsthand. Repressive ash surrounded the walls, plunged over, and filled the city. Then the sulfur storm came. Flames whizzed through the air like blue bullets, struck the ground, and ignited on impact. Nasal passages and throats burned from caustic precipitation. Sodomites struggled to breathe. Those who remained outside darted for cover, but most never made it. Instead, they shrieked as sulfur rain pelted their bodies.

Blue flames ignited clothes on contact. Women wailed as falling sulfur scorched their bodies, melting their skin like ice at the equator. Candle-wax flesh dripped from their bones onto screaming children clinging to their mothers' legs. Men attempted to usher the women and children indoors, but most dropped to their knees and cursed the dark sky above as it devoured them. People of all ages lay screaming and dying in the streets, tortured by burning flesh and sulfur air. Screams turned to gasps as sulfur replaced oxygen in their lungs. Skeletons crumpled to the ground. In ditches running beside Sodom's main streets, molten yellow rivers formed with blue flames dancing on top.

Those who could still stand hurled themselves into the burning floes to end the nightmare immediately. Trees and dwellings ignited as the cloud lurched forward, leaving a fiery swath in its wake. When the mass reached the southern wall, a chorus of hellish screams could be heard, as the Sodomites who fled were scorched and asphyxiated before the south gate could be opened.

Teodor remained on the mountain until nearly noon. Sulfur killed all the miners who had stayed, yet it never affected him. The fires started to recede from the time Teodor began incantations, only by that point it was too late for Sodom. After a few hours of singing and casting spells, the fires ceased completely. Though the mountain still simmered, Teodor lowered the temperature inside so no more sulfur ignited. When he was satisfied, he gathered the miners' bodies on a cart for hauling sulfur and headed back to Sodom.

After the hissing mass passed the mortuary, an eerie glow set in. A putrid, yellowish-caked mustard-like mist blocked the sun. Sulfur showers had ceased, and though the mist remained, I put on a coat, hat, and gloves and stepped outside. The grisly scene spread before me: bodies scattered around in peculiar postures, piles of scorched bones, little blue fires burning along the street. Mustard mist hung around, an overbearing authority that didn't affect my breathing. Still, from Fifth and Sixth, sounds of The Captives' carnival roared.

I wheeled the cart into the street and piled corpses on top, lugged it back to the mortuary where I lined the bodies up and tagged the toes. After the fifth such trip, I noticed a gang parading through the streets as if in celebration. When they approached, the leader, dressed like a circus announcer, veered over to me and whispered, "You can breathe just as we do" and returned to his position. The group filtered by, talked, and giggled as they hopped over dead bodies without honoring them. The one bringing up the rear, dressed as a nine-tailed kitty cat, came over to me and said, "Captives own this town," then he returned to his position. At the time, I didn't notice the casket hovering in the middle of the throng as they continued down the street toward the north gate.

Teodor met the parade outside the north gate where they welcomed him like a war hero. Screams of excitement and indecipherable incantations filled the air. Fire shot high into the grey sky and lit up northern Sodom despite the sulfur gloom. They played music with their instruments, clapped, and sang until roaring applause erupted. When the celebration mellowed, the crowd entered the city and proclaimed Teodor as Sodom's king. They paraded down the street, whooping and singing, dancing, and shouting. With Teodor leading and the levitating casket enshrouded by the crowd, the throng headed for the mortuary.

The day was certainly busy for a mortician. As the sulfur mass moved past Sodom and over open plains, I continued tagging bodies. Soon, the Sodomites who had survived began to appear on the streets. Although they had witnessed the carnage through peepholes, the brunt of the catastrophe was only understood firsthand. They gawked at piles of bones, skin still burning, skeletons crumpled in the streets, and vomited at the smell of sizzled flesh. Slowly, they identified family and friends, dropped to their knees, and wailed in the street. They began showing up at the mortuary and lined up single file at the side door. Generations of superstition prevented them from entering, as dwellings that housed the dead were considered unclean in Sodom. I handed out toe tags and promised to pick up the bodies as soon as possible. Those who couldn't find their loved ones in the streets sifted through the corpses laid out in rows behind the mortuary. Wives slumped and cried over husbands. Mothers and fathers wailed over children. Men hunched against walls and sobbed. The mortuary yard was flooded with tears.

Teodor interrupted the chaos when he cut in line and pounded on the door. The grieving dried their eyes and turned their attention to him. When he showed them the cartful of bodies from the mountain, they realized he was the Fire Starter.

"Told you not to set those fires!" one of the old-timers shouted.

Mayor Bera and Sheriff Hammu approached Teodor, threatened to arrest him, or worse. But before they accosted him, he redirected blame to the Miners' Council. "I warned the Council not to set more fires, but they approved the measure anyway. They threatened to kill me if I didn't comply."

The crowd seemed to believe him, as Teodor wielded strange power over the will of Sodom's people.

Mayor Bera doubted Teodor's claim. He stepped onto the curb and shouted, "Why, Sodomites, do you believe this stranger? This leader of a captive people?"

No one listened to him. Their attention was aimed at Teodor.

"Unfortunately," Teodor informed them, "All the members of the Council perished on the mountain." He pointed to the cart. "Their bodies lay on this cart."

"He blames the dead who cannot defend themselves," Mayor Bera said. "How do we know the truth?"

Sodomite men rushed to the cart and tossed miner bodies aside as they searched for Council members. They pulled each of the five members off the cart and piled the corpses in the street.

Sheriff Hammu stood on the curb and announced, "These five men—the Miners' Council—caused the blast this morning. They don't deserve a proper burial! They deserve to burn in the street like other Sodomites did!"

A deputy in the crowd left to find fuel as momentum toward torching the bodies grew. During the rush, Teodor ducked inside the mortuary. The deputy returned with a container of ethanol. Another deputy grabbed it and doused the bodies. Sheriff Hammu continued, "Let the orange fire consume these wicked bastards, those who brought the blue flames upon our fair city!"

I pushed the cart of bodies around the corner as a sulfur chunk ignited and dropped atop the pile. "Why must you disrespect the dead?" I demanded, approaching the throng of Sodomites.

"These are your people, fellow citizens of Sodom!" Sheriff Hammu scoffed from the curb. "Someone must pay!"

"What revenge is torching dead bodies?" I asked.

"The bodies must be torched to avenge the Sodomites who died in fiery agony!"

"Why continue the carnage?"

His expression changed. "You're the mortician. Yes, I'm seeing it clearly now. The man who earns his living among the dead. You want the bodies whole, fresh, so you can charge us for funerals! You just want our money like the bloody Captives!"

Sheriff Hammu's tone sent a chill up my spine.

"I'm not a greedy man," I said and ducked into the mortuary to avoid escalation. As the door closed, the crowd pushed towards it. I feared they would break it down.

Once inside, I found Teodor waiting for me in the vestibule. He was sitting in a calm pose with eyes closed until he realized I stood before him. A wooden coffin, decorated with immaculate carvings of mammoth animals and men of equal height, floated next to him, hovering at my waist level.

A strange glint flashed in Teodor's eyes when they opened. "Just the man I want to see," he said, as I stared at the coffin. "I hauled some bodies from the mountain, and then we have this one."

His eyebrows motioned to the coffin, though his gaze stayed fixed on me.

"I'll see to the bodies you hauled down," I responded, pointing to the casket. "But what service can I provide for this? Who's in there?"

"You're a man who gets straight to the point," he replied. "I like you already. Most would ask how it hovers there." He stood and circled the casket. "The prowess showcased each night at Sixth and Seventh, that's what hovers before you. As legend foretold, he died the day the mountain erupted, over a thousand years since his birth on the day the mountain last raged."

I'd heard rumors around Sodom that The Captives lived to untold ages. Some claimed many hundreds of years, in fact, but no one ever claimed a thousand until Teodor. I decided not to question him since I didn't know exactly what he wanted.

"So, what do you want from me?" I inquired.

As the question left my mouth, someone pounded the door, rattling the windows.

"We know you're in there!" Sheriff Hammu announced. "And the Fire Starter too. Come on out!"

Teodor and I exchanged glances, but neither of us knew what to do. I peeked out the window to see the angry Sodomites surrounding the mortuary.

Just down the street, The Captives danced and sang while waiting for Teodor to finish his business. One of them warned the Sodomite crowd to leave the mortician alone or risk invoking the spirits residing at the mortuary. The Sodomites moved toward The Captives, cursing them for devilish magic and threatened violence if they didn't disburse at once.

They continued dancing and singing, refusing to leave. One of the Sodomites raised a knife. The crowd roared and a melee ensued.

Captives warded off blows with shifting feet and other swift movements. But sheer Sodomite numbers overwhelmed them. Blows landed on heads and sternums. Sodomites pounded Captives, slit throats, and dropped bodies. Heads were bashed, chests ripped open, and rivers of blood flowed in the street. Only a dozen or so Captives remained alive.

Teodor showed anxiety, a nervousness I hadn't seen displayed by any of The Captives. He turned to me with panicked eyes and said, "Like me, the sulfur air didn't affect your breathing. The blue flames never burned one sore into your skin. Don't you find it remarkable?" He urged me to look out the window.

Outside, the gang of Sodomites stood over The Captives, who were still alive. Each Sodomite body displayed sulfur wounds, from open sores to singed skin to bloody noses. But signs of sulfur affliction were absent from The Captives. And as I checked out mine and Teodor's skin, I realized neither of us showed wounds, either. I rubbed my hands together and placed them on my face. My skin still felt soft.

"See?" he asked. "No wounds, no sores, no burns." He inhaled deeply.

I looked at him through my fingers.

"Why don't you save your people?" I demanded. "Use your magic to save them."

He shuffled his feet and sat up straight. "These are not my people. It's true that sulfur doesn't affect them as it does the Sodomites, but they are not my people."

The answer confused me. "But you lived among them. They revere you."

He stood and peered out the window. The crowd of Sodomites had surrounded the mortuary again.

"Straight to the point," Teodor whirled to face me. "I was sent by Kedorlaomer."

The crowd outside chunked rocks at the mortuary walls. Then, another pounding shook the door.

"One more chance!" Sheriff Hammu announced. "Bring us the mortician. Or bring us the Fire Starter. Or bring us both!"

The last demand raised excitement in the growing crowd, which applauded and hollered its approval.

"You see," Teodor said, "To the Sodomites, we are one and the same. They don't care which one of us comes out, only that they receive a sacrificial lamb. But one will not satisfy vengeance. If one of us comes out, they will string him up, lynch him in the street. Soon, the taste of blood will fade, and they will return to demand the other."

"Kedorlaomer sent you?" I asked.

"Yes; when captives were released, many set off for Sodom. Kedorlaomer instructed me to blend in with them. He had developed a plan to take Sodom down. My job was to enchant the captives, those the Sodomites call 'Strangers', and once we arrived in Sodom, to direct The Captives into enchanting Sodom's residents."

"Why are you telling me all of this? I'm a Sodomite."

"Indeed, you dwell in Sodom. You're also familiar with magic and illusion. You work with the dead. It's your business."

"What do you want from me?" I asked him.

"What I seek is survival. Angry Sodomites stand outside the door, waiting to tear us limb from limb."

"How can I help you survive if they kill me also?"

"Here in the mortuary, we are safe. They may threaten, but Sodomites won't dare enter a dwelling of the dead."

"So, we stay here until the crowd disperses?"

"Not exactly. Who can say how long the crowd will remain? When people are racked by grief and vengeance, they do unnatural things."

"So, you're saying we're trapped here?"

He darted his eyes toward the coffin and back at me.

"The casket?"

He nodded and smiled.

"And how will a floating casket save us both?"

He lifted a finger and straightened his spine. "Kedorlaomer sent the casket with me and The Captives. As I said, it's the origin of the magic displayed in Sodom since we arrived. We enchanted Sodom with a corpse, even though Sodomites refuse to confront death on purpose. Yet they came to the carnival every night and ignored the casket hovering stage left." He paused to peek through the window. "Regardless of how inflamed the crowd becomes, they won't dare approach a casket, especially one that hovers above the ground, for fear of invoking wrath from the dead spirit."

"So, your plan is that we both climb into the coffin and float down the street?"

"Well, one of us will climb into the coffin," he replied. "But there's more to the plan." He drew a deep breath before continuing. "Last night, Kedorlaomer sent two men into Sodom. They warned people that the mountain would explode, sulfur would rain down on the city, and many people would die. The Sodomites laughed at the men, threatened them with violence and sexual depravity as The Captives had modeled for them."

"Why would Kedorlaomer warn Sodom if he wants to control it?"

"He doesn't care about Sodom. Kedorlaomer wants the sulfur mines, and control of the black gunpowder trade. He gave Sodom a chance to save itself."

"Good for Kedorlaomer. But how does it help us escape?"

"The two men who Kedorlaomer sent last night, the ones chased off by the Sodomites, are waiting for us where the road from Sodom forks to Zoar and Zeboyim. The Captives will escort us to the north gate, and none of the Sodomites will dare approach. All we must do is find those two men. They will handle the rest."

Sheriff Hammu's voice thundered from outside, interrupting Teodor, "Last chance! This time I mean it! Either come out or we set the mortuary ablaze!"

The crowd cheered. Flickers of torches danced through the windows.

Teodor grabbed my shoulder with a grip weaker than I imagined it would be. "The crowd smolders; we must proceed! Make an announcement, keep them from setting fire. I need a few minutes alone."

"What are you talking about? Your life is threatened, and you need a few minutes alone?"

"Exactly. This day needs magic if we are to survive." He stood up and walked to the back of the room, peered inside my office. "May I sit in here?"

For some reason, I began to trust this Teodor. Plus, he was the only ally I had at the moment. "Go ahead, if that's what you need to do."

"Keep the crowd at bay. Tell them you must deliver a body across town. I'll take care of the rest. Won't be long."

He ducked into the office and shut the door.

I peeked out the window. Angry men surrounded the mortuary, though they remained a safe distance away. Their women and children ducked behind them, shot snarls at me. Some of the men talked among themselves, others brandished blades. But what frightened me were the men holding torches, and I figured ethanol was on the way. As Teodor said, Sodomites would never enter the mortuary. But in their rage, they would burn it down even if it instigated the spirits.

The sheriff and mayor stood in front of the group.

"What say you, mortician?" Mayor Bera hollered.

"I need to come out soon," I replied.

"Will you sacrifice your own life to save the Fire Starter?" Mayor Bera asked.

"Bring him to us and save yourself!" Sheriff Hammu demanded.

"I have a coffin that needs delivering to the other side of town."

They looked perplexed. Mayor Bera whispered to Sheriff Hammu, who nodded and turned a hostile eye towards me.

"We will allow you to pass with the casket," Mayor Bera said.

"But we will follow, and once the body's dropped off, you're ours!" Sheriff Hammu hollered.

"I'm the only man in Sodom who can give your dead a proper burial," I shouted back. "Not too smart to murder me."

They spoke to each other again.

"You speak truth, mortician. Only for the spirits of the recently departed will we spare your life," Mayor Bera said.

"For now," Sheriff Hammu said. "In that case, we demand the Fire Starter!"

As the words left Sheriff Hammu's mouth, a sonic boom rattled Sodom. The ground rumbled and groaned. The mortuary walls shook. As I ducked away, the second window shattered. Men crouched and flung arms over their heads. Women dropped to the ground, screaming. Children covered their ears. Shrieks and cries echoed in the streets, reverberating through alleyways. A woman stumbled by, repeating, "This day is cursed! This day is cursed!" Sodom's survivors were growing weary, but they had another obstacle to overcome.

Teodor opened the office door and strolled to the coffin.

"Are you refreshed?" I asked him.

"Yes, I needed that," he replied as he ran fingers along the carvings.

"What did you do in there?"

"Didn't you hear the explosion?"

"Of course, I did. It shattered the window!"

He smiled at me.

"Wait, you caused it?"

He smiled wider.

"How'd you do that?" I asked.

"Magic, my friend. A little concentrated magic. Sodomites could learn a lot about focused intention. Soon, the cloud will rise again and bear down on Sodom. Soon, the crowd will disperse. Soon, we make our escape."

He walked to the window and stuck his head out. The men were standing, brushing off. He spoke.

"Listen up, residents of Sodom! You call for our heads, the mortician and the Fire Starter. But you misunderstand what's happening here. It's true that sulfur caused the destruction earlier today. But not from my fires! Two visitors came to Sodom last night and warned of impending destruction. They claimed to be messengers from Shinab, king of Admah. They said Sodom is brimming with evil, corrupted by the Captives, unworthy to pillage the sulfur mines."

Teodor lowered his voice and said to me, "They believe Shinab is a sorcerer, and all attacks attributed to him are the result of black magic."

The Sodomites looked at each other as they brushed off. A group of men stepped toward Mayor Bera and Sheriff Hammu, backing up Teodor's claim.

They had witnessed two dark-cloaked men confronting people headed to the carnival the previous night. The men stood on the curb hollering about vengeance and judgment, questioning Sodom's moral fortitude, cursing as the crowds passed without paying attention. Everyone figured them to be drunken tourists.

This went on well into the evening. As midnight approached, one of the men stood on a curb and made an announcement. "We offered you a chance, Sodom! Yet not one of you heeded us! The hour is at hand, Sodom!"

Sodomites who had witnessed the display laughed and threw sticks and rocks at him. The man jumped off the curb and joined the other. They pulled hoods over their heads and slunk toward the north gate. Other men agreed they, too, had seen these men but didn't realize what was going on at the time. Whispers spread through the crowd about what they missed while at the carnival the previous night.

"There's more, good people of Sodom!" Teodor exclaimed. He waited for the crowd's full attention and continued. "Last night, I saw those two men on the road to the mountain. I begged them not to destroy Sodom. But they said my pleas were useless. At dawn, Shinab would detonate the mountain. I did what I could to stop it, residents of Sodom! This is the work of Shinab of Admah!"

Another boom rocked Sodom. The crowd shuddered in unison. This blast was unlike the previous ones, which were powerful, no doubt, but sounded more like mining accidents. This one dwarfed those. It was the grand finale: I knew the mountain had blown its top. Putrid smells wafted down the street. A strange glow emanated from the mountain, yellow bile with blue flames following closely behind. Rancid sulfur air approached the north gate.

Teodor stepped out the door to finish the ruse. "I see Shinab's not done yet, Sodomites! Prepare for sulfur rain! Take cover, good people of Sodom! Save yourselves!" He ducked back inside and winked at me as sulfur chunks began to fall and burst into blue flames. "Let's get out of this forsaken town."

Outside, the Sodomites scurried for cover. They'd survived the earlier onslaught but realized this one was even greater. Destruction surely loomed.

The Captives who survived the melee rose to their feet and cranked up a street party. As the day's second sulfur cloud enveloped the city, they played their strange instruments and sang and danced, though their numbers had dwindled to less than a dozen.

I began preparing for the second onslaught of sulfur. The first one had devastated the town; the second would destroy it. Teodor ignored the threat and stood over the casket, his eyes closed, and mumbled under his breath. When he was finished, he raised his head and spoke to me. "Are you prepared to leave this town?"

"I'm ready to avoid the sulfur storm," I said as I blocked the windows with furniture.

"Don't waste your time," he advised. "After we leave this mortuary and pass through the north gate, Sodom will be destroyed. You will never see it again as it stands now." He motioned me to join him beside the casket. I noticed a soft hum vibrating from it. "You're comfortable with the dead. Until now, you made your living preparing bodies for proper burial so the souls may fly free from this decrepit world."

I nodded in agreement, though I failed to recognize his angle.

"Yes, I'm a mortician, as my father was before me and his father before him. My family has served Sodom for seven generations. We've cleansed and prepared thousands of bodies, buried or cremated them in preparation for the journey to higher realms."

"And now, you will do the same for me."

I looked at him through confused eyes. "What do you mean? You're not dead."

"Oh, mortician! So accustomed to seeing spirits that he no longer separates the dead from those with hearts still beating!"

Teodor extended an arm and summoned my hand with his fingers. He pressed my hand against his cloak. Inside his chest, no heart pounded; stillness and silence filled the cavity.

"Not what you expected?"

"But, if you're dead, how do you stand before me?"

My mind raced for answers. He drew a deep breath.

I paced as blue flames whistled down on Sodom. People in the street slumped in agony, begged for mercy. Deafening thunder answered their pleas as sizzling bolts lit up the street. Flames engulfed entire blocks of row houses and shops. Curdling screams pierced the air before bodies were vaporized by putrid mist. Some dove for cover only to land in other fires. Blue flames engulfed the city as if all things touched by Sodomites were sentenced to spontaneous combustion.

"Death is but an illusion," Teodor finally said, "as I'm sure you've realized in your occupation. Bodies are concentrated energy, manifestations of the spirits sailing through this realm. Those who understand magic and the connection between earth and sky recognize the sheer veil between life and death. The body is nothing more than an animated vehicle for the spirit. It provides depth and limitation to explore and learn. And as the spirit advances down the road, it, too, understands the gift the body provides, but also the lack of necessity for it."

He raised his eyebrows and glanced at the casket. "Are you ready to see who's inside?"

I nodded, though unsure if I was ready. He released the latches, paused before opening the heavy top.

"See you on the other side," he said as he inhaled deeply and opened the casket. Inside, lying in a silk suit the likes of which no Sodomite had witnessed in generations, was a body and face that looked exactly like Teodor's.

I stared at the corpse in disbelief. But when I returned my glance to the identical body standing beside me, it had changed. Instead of a vibrant man, the body appeared weakened. I saw waves of energy flowing through it, like the humidity one sees in desert mirages.

"Remember to breathe," he said.

Teodor's body became translucent, and I could see through it to the walls behind. In seconds, the mirage disappeared. Only Teodor the corpse remained. My body flinched, and my lip snarled. I slammed the casket closed. I tried to shake it off and sat down to catch my breath.

I've experienced strange moments as a mortician, but nothing to this extreme. Never before had I seen two identical bodies—one dead, the other alive—in the same moment. High magic indeed, perhaps grander than the fire starting on the mountain.

I wondered who this Teodor really was. He claimed the corpse in the casket was over a thousand years old. But he also claimed to be sent by Kedorlaomer, the man Sodomites reviled more than any other. More than Shinab, even. Perplexing questions for a simple mortician, and ones that would have to wait until a more suitable time.

I gathered important papers, stuffed them in a satchel, and slung the satchel over my shoulder. I hurried from the office to peer out the window. Yellow haze dominated the view. Blue flames danced in random places. When I turned back to the vestibule, I noticed a funny thing—the casket was hovering right behind me, as if it had followed me to the window. I walked back to the office and the casket followed.

I walked to the window. Again, it followed. Another extreme moment, another crest of strangeness in a day full of oddities.

When I stepped outside, the casket trailed behind me. Thunder boomed, lightning sizzled, blue flames rained down and connected with fires already burning. Moaning and wailing pierced the sulfur air from piles of flesh and bone along the street. Two bodies staggered ten feet in front of me and collapsed into the fog. The Sodomite throng was decimated, their bodies crumpled on the ground.

I inhaled deeply. Off to my right, I heard sounds of The Captives celebrating, though I couldn't see them through the fog. Their instruments and voices no longer sounded so strange but welcoming and protective. My confidence grew; my body stood tall, my shoulders settled. I stepped on a corpse. When I bent down, Sheriff Hammu's charbroiled face stared at me. His body collapsed as if imploding. I vomited on his melted badge. After wiping my mouth and adjusting the satchel over my shoulder, I crept through the fog towards The Captives, careful to avoid stepping on other corpses. The casket hovered behind me like a dog following its master.

When I reached The Captives dancing and singing and playing in the street, the fog parted, as if I stepped through a door into a sparkling room. A spotlight shined on me, though sunlight was blocked by sulfur, and I figured it to be close to dusk, anyway. The Captives welcomed me like a lost hero. They flung arms in the air, exchanged hugs, and focused big smiles with the force of their clapping hands.

The one dressed like a circus announcer quieted the rest. Then he leaned towards me and said, "Follow me."

The rest of The Captives encircled me and the casket. They continued dancing and singing and playing their instruments as we moved, parade style, down the street behind the ringmaster. Mustard fog hung thickly around the circle's edge. Inside, the perimeter was clear, the air clean and crisp, like my personal vehicle marching through Sodom's decay and madness. The parade synced to the melody of the strange instruments and maneuvered around dead bodies with grace. Sodomites still clinging to life coughed and moaned and pled for help as we passed. Bony arms with melted skin reached up from the ground, but The Captives smashed the shoulders with heavy boots and the parade continued moving until it reached Sodom's north gate.

Once outside the gate, the circle widened, and the ringmaster stepped to the middle. The rest of The Captives gathered behind him. He removed his tall hat and bowed to me. The rest followed his lead. After a few moments, he raised his head and said, "The hour is at hand. After today, Sodom is ours! Now it burns, but soon, it shall be known as the greatest of the cities of the plains! Never shall we forget the grace and fortitude of Teodorlaomer!"

The Captives roared behind him. They commenced a raucous tune and seductive dancing. The circus announcer leaned close to my ear and said, "Here begins the road to Zoar." He pointed to the charred path extending into the gloom and then turned to join the celebration.

I watched The Captives filter back into Sodom through the north gate. Drifts of fog hung around me, and blue fires burned intermittently in the grasses surrounding the road. But nothing as thick as inside the city walls. I turned to Sodom for a final look, realizing I would never return. A tear dribbled down my cheek as I took the first step toward Zoar, casket in tow: the mortician abandoning his city.

The cloud enshrouded Sodom, shot lightning inside the walls, and hurled blue fire to the buildings and streets. The city crackled and a sickly fluorescence glowed from inside. Caustic rain poured within the walls, and sulfur ash floated in the air outside.

I brushed particulates from my face and turned towards Zoar. As I walked down the road, a series of explosions rattled the Jordan Valley, each one growing in volume and intensity. Sodom, as I knew it, no longer existed. A new chapter would begin, one written by The Captives.

As I neared the fork in the road, one way leading to Zoar, the other to Zeboyim, the fog lifted, and the night sky opened. A half-moon hung low in the west and stars shimmered in a way I'd never before noticed. At the fork, I sat on a stump to rest my legs and admire the sky. The casket hovered beside me. As I gazed at stars, two silhouettes appeared from the trees. At first, they approached like shadows, and I thought my mind was playing tricks on me. As they moved closer, I realized two men—tall forms covered with dark cloaks—approached. I positioned myself between them and the casket.

"Fear not," the taller one said. "I am Baal, this is Molech." They bowed. "We greet you in friendship. You're the mortician, no?"

"I was the mortician of Sodom," I replied and placed a hand in my coat pocket to appear as if carrying a weapon. "But Sodom is no more."

"Teodor said you would meet us here," Molech said, "and that you would deliver the casket to us."

We all laid eyes on the casket.

"As you can see, the casket is safe and sound."

"Do you know who's in the casket?" Baal asked.

"Yes, I do." I placed a hand on the top of it. "I watched the man climb in with my own eyes."

"Good," Molech responded. "So, you understand the importance of delivering the casket to Zoar safely?"

"I understood the importance of escaping Sodom with my life."

"And now, here you are, free from the wrath cast upon Sodom."

"Yes, here I am."

"Now your task is accomplished. We shall handle the casket from here. Your service is greatly appreciated," the two said in unison, bowing.

I returned a bow and watched them whispering in each other's ears. After a few moments, Baal spoke. "Bandits often roam the road between here and Zoar. It's best if you travel with us."

Molech shouldered my satchel, and we set off toward Zoar. For what seemed like days, we walked, with Baal and Molech on either side of the casket and me behind. Twice we saw shadows on the road ahead, but they vanished by the time we reached the spot. We neared Zoar by sunrise without threat from bandits.

As we approached, the main gate opened and a man with two guards ushered us inside. No one stared or even blinked at the casket, as if it was invisible. He introduced himself as Nefi. In silence, he led us past vendors setting up stalls. Two guards followed. After navigating two streets, we turned into an alley and ducked into a wooden building. Inside, candles flickered, revealing the dirt floor and stone walls.

"The casket shall rest here," Nefi said, and signaled the two guards to post beside it.

He motioned me, Baal, and Molech up a stairway in the corner. It opened into an exquisite dwelling with gold fixtures, plush carpets, and exotic decorations. Servants were the only people visible, and they performed their tasks without lifting their gazes to acknowledge us.

"You men must be worn out," Nefi said with a snicker. "We've prepared a room for each of you."

We followed him up corkscrewing stairs until we reached the sixth floor, where we stepped into a long corridor with many doors. Candles cast the only light from fixtures on each door frame. Nefi stopped at the first two rooms and motioned Molech and Baal inside. They bid us good day and closed the doors behind them.

"Mighty warriors, those two," he said as we continued down the corridor before stopping in front of a double door. "And here is your room, sir." He bowed. "The mortician. Never thought we'd see you again." He smiled and bowed again before pushing the doors open.

Before me spread an immaculate room: a lapis floor with wall hangings of Persian cloth, Chinese silk, and an ancient mandala formed by shiny jewels.

"Do you remember?" he asked as he whirled me around to face a mirror, a decoration I hadn't seen since childhood. "Look!" he demanded.

When I peered into the mirror, I saw something strange, or rather, something familiar. I'd seen the face that stared back at me the previous day in Sodom, in fact. It was the face of Teodor, the face of the corpse, the same being I saw at once standing beside me and laying dead in the casket. The same being I watched dissipate before my eyes. I felt nauseous and vomited on the floor.

"Don't worry. I'll get it cleaned up. No shame in moments of such revelation."

"Teodor and I, we have the same face," I said in a low voice.

"Of course, you do!"

I felt nauseous again but fought the urge. Confusion cascaded over me. "But Teodor's in the casket. He was walking around yesterday, but also in the casket."

"Yes, yes, he was," Nefi agreed.

"But how do I have the same face? How do I share a face with a dead man? A mad man! A magician!"

Nefi snickered. "You don't share a face. You shared a womb."

"What? What are you talking about?"

"You and Teodor were identical twins. Sons of Kedorlaomer and Naomi. Nine hundred years ago, you were sent by the Seer to Sodom to tend the mortuary and the spirits residing there. All those years you waited, perhaps you forgot why you were even there. But you waited, because deep down you knew that one day your identical twin brother would come along needing your help. And the Seer was correct. On that day, Kedorlaomer's power was consolidated, and Sodom destroyed."

He handed me an envelope with a red seal and said, "Get some rest. When you wake, the rest of the princes shall be here."

"Rest of the princes?" I asked.

He smiled and pointed to the envelope. "Answers to all your questions await you." Nefi extinguished the candle on the mantle and walked toward the door. "Welcome home," he said, closing the door.

My fingers caressed the red wax. *The Seer?*

I deciphered the Kedorlaomer seal on the envelope. *Identical brother Teodor?*

I ripped open the envelope. On yellowed paper, a note was scribbled:

'Dear Fedor,

If you're reading this, you escaped Sodom and arrived in Zoar. Welcome home, Son! Your time at the mortuary is over, the role played to perfection. Your brothers will arrive this afternoon, nine hundred years since you've all been together. Tonight, we celebrate! Family loyalty, dedication and sacrifice, victory over the cities of the plain! Rest easy and prepare to feast at dusk. Today, you shall remember!

Your Father, Kedor'

Remember what?

My mind raced, eyes bulged, limbs shook. *All my brothers? Mortician role played to perfection? One thousand years?* I vomited again.

Kedorlaomer, my father?

My joints froze and my chest went numb. I flopped onto the bed. Contrary voices argued between my ears. I flipped through memories of Sodom—the long days at the mortuary with Luka, the simple life before the Battle of the Vale, the change introduced by The Captives.

The rest of the princes shall be here!

My body shot straight up, my eyelids stretched wide. The facade cracked, and I remembered.

Images flooded into my mind as I stared at the bejeweled mandala on the wall: I sat in a candle-lit room around the oak table with my seven brothers; my father Kedorlaomer and his advisors huddled at the head. From under his cloak, the Seer predicted Sodom's dominance over black gunpowder. My father leaned into the candlelight as he explained the plan: infiltrate the cities of Jordan's plain, blend in and wait until the sulfur mines can be controlled. Nefi the Magician, the same man who led me from the gate to this room, poured each of us a potion. "This will help you forget. At all times, you will only remember the previous forty years," he told me. By morning, the bitter liquid changed me from prince and astrologer to mortician. The mission required I work in Sodom away from my brothers, my family, my home. I traveled there with my faithful servant Luka, who posed as my father to strengthen the ruse. I gladly drank the potion. *Who wants to remember such a sacrifice?*

Nine hundred years ago, we sat around the table. Yesterday, I woke as The Mortician of Sodom. Yesterday, my twin Teodorlaomer destroyed Sodom with its own sulfur mountain. Today, my father's kingdom rules over Sodom and the other cities of the plain, and I remember my life as prince and astrologer. Tonight, Nefi raises Teodor from the otherworld. Tonight, I will be reunited with seven brothers.

A grin grew across my face, my arms spread wide, and I announced, "I am Fedorlaomer, eldest son of Kedorlaomer, King of the Jordan River Valley."

I vomited on the floor again, dry heaved twice through a smile, then closed my eyes and drifted to royal dreams.

STARLIGHT

Erin Vataris

Geula was afraid of the dark. She was afraid of the shadows that oozed out of the brick walls in the middle of the night and piled on the floor near her bed, thick and deep, waiting for her to step into them. She was afraid of the sound of the wind as it whistled past the windows in the darkness. She was afraid of the sound of the baked bricks cooling, the tick and crackle of the mortar between them. But most of all, she was afraid of the black empty dark.

Sometimes, when she hung her feet over the edges of the bed, the darkness climbed up them and made them disappear until she pulled them up and found them again. Sometimes, in the middle of the night, especially on the black dark nights when the clouds covered the stars and there was no moon, she thought she could feel it climbing up the side of the sleeping ledge, seeping into her sleeping mat and trying to make all of her disappear.

Geula didn't want to disappear. She didn't want the dark to eat her, so she stayed still on her mat and closed her eyes so she couldn't see how dark it was. She squeezed them closed so tightly that the darkness couldn't leak in, and then she pushed her fingers against her eyelids until she could see bright flashing spots even after she opened them again.

She did it again and again until she couldn't see the darkness anymore, then sometimes she could sleep, but the darkness was still there. It was waiting for her to fall asleep so it could climb up the ledge and into her mat and eat her all gone.

Her legs hurt from where Immi had whipped her for falling asleep at the loom yesterday, so she wiggled them a little bit. Not much, or the mat would crackle and the darkness would know she was there. Her lungs hurt from trying not to breathe too loudly. Her eyes hurt from pushing on them. But she was still there. It hadn't gotten her yet. Geula tried to think about staying awake, but she was so tired. She just wanted to go to sleep. She wished they would let her leave a lamp on, but oil was more precious than one silly little girl's silly little fears.

Abbi had put an altar in the alcove of the sleeping room for her and traded Immi's fine-woven linens for a statue of Asherah with a bronze crown that glittered. He sighed the whole while, but he put Asherah in the altar where the moonlight could shine in the window and catch her crown.

Asherah was a fine goddess to protect her. Geula knew that. She knew that Abbi gave her an altar and not another whipping because he loved her, just like Immi had whipped Geula's legs out of love and didn't want her to ruin a whole length of cloth by falling asleep and tangling the shuttle so it had to be all unwoven. Geula knew that.

When the moon shone in and the bronze crown sent stars dancing over the walls of the alcove, Geula could almost see Asherah moving. She could feel the goddess's gaze on her while she shifted and pushed on her eyes and tried to sleep, and Geula was almost as afraid of that as she was of the shadows that filled up the alcove on cloudy nights. On cloudy nights—nights like tonight—she couldn't see Asherah at all. She could just hear her moving in the darkness, and she knew, just as surely as she knew the darkness wanted to swallow her up, that Asherah was moving.

Asherah lived in the statue in the altar in the alcove, and Geula wasn't quite sure whether Asherah wanted to help her or beat her for her childishness.

Asherah never helped her. She just stood there being stone and bronze during the daytime, and at night she roamed around her alcove where the altar was, eating the olives and honey milk they left for her and trying to get out. Sometimes on the darkest nights, the nights with no moon, Geula could hear her feet like raindrops, and she wondered what would happen if Asherah got out.

Those were the worst nights, where she lay on her mat and shivered, afraid of the darkness, afraid of Asherah. Those were the nights when she was so afraid that she couldn't even make herself get up to pee, and she would lay in bed afraid until it all came spilling out of her in a hot wet stream that dried on her legs and made her mat stink. She got whipped when that happened, a big girl like her peeing in her bed, and Immi made her carry her own mat down to the river, heavy and reeking, to wash it. That was bad, but on the worst nights the darkness was worse than whippings. It was worse than washing her mat. It was worse than everything.

#

Usually, Geula went to pee before she went to bed, especially on this kind of night, because having to wash her mat was bad, and whippings were worse, but on this night, something was wrong even before bedtime. Even Geula knew something was wrong. It had started with dinner alone with Immi because Abbi had gone to a meeting. Immi was so angry that she'd left his lamb stew to sit on the table and get thick and gloppy until the fat was a cold yellow skin over the top. It was all right to go to meetings, but it wasn't all right to miss dinner for them. Not in this house.

It had been later than late when Abbi finally came home, and so dark that the shadows were starting to pool up in the corners of the main room. He was never that late. He'd come stumbling in the front door, holding the frame for balance and moving like he couldn't see where he was going. Immi had called him Ephraim in her angry voice, and Abbi turned his face toward her, and his eyes had been white— like sand or clouds on a hot day, filmy and pale.

"Ephraim!"

Immi had said it again, then she was crying and holding Abbi's face. They were talking in grown-up language, the kind that sounded nice but looked like fighting, and Geula didn't know what was wrong. She wanted to know why Abbi's eyes looked like that, and she wanted to know what happened to make him so late, but then Immi told her to go to bed, and she used *that* voice.

When Immi used *that* voice, Geula went, and she knew better than to mention the way the shadows were reaching out of the walls to get her. She just went, and she got in her bed by hopping over the shadow lines in the tile. And then Geula laid on her mat and listened to the sounds of voices on the other side of the wall and stared at Asherah while she waited for the darkness to fill up the whole room.

Asherah never moved when Geula could see her, and she always was careful to stand in the same spot when the morning came and pushed the darkness aside. But why would you leave food out for a statue if it wasn't alive?

Geula knew that when she wasn't looking, Asherah got up and moved around and ate the food and drank the milk they left for her. It was gone in the mornings. So, she laid on her mat and watched Asherah so Asherah wouldn't wake up and start moving, and that was when she realized she hadn't gone pee. She hadn't gone pee, and now the darkness had covered the whole floor and Geula would have to step in it to go.

Immi and Abbi were still talking in the other room. She could hear them, and the way their voices weren't quite so whispery anymore, but she didn't understand what they were saying. Something about strangers.

There were always strangers. They came to buy and sell and trade. Geula didn't understand why these strangers were so important. She didn't understand what they had to do with the sand clouds in Abbi's eyes. She blinked her eyes a few times, wondering if Abbi's eyes felt scratchy, like sand, like hers did in the morning after holding them open all night long. She blinked and rubbed her eyes, and then she froze.

Asherah had moved.

Geula was sure that before she'd rubbed her eyes, Asherah had her left foot forward. Now her right one was forward, or maybe it was the other way around, but it had been the other foot.

She'd only blinked once, and Asherah had moved. Except that when she'd closed her eyes, Immi and Abbi were talking in the eating room, and now they weren't. They were in this room, sleeping.

She could see them, lumps of darkness in the shadows. She could hear Abbi snoring and Immi's little whistling breaths, sleeping deep and uncaring that an eyeblink ago they had been talking with the tallow lamplight making wiggling flickers of safety through the doorway.

She'd fallen asleep. Geula had fallen asleep rubbing her eyes, and she'd stopped watching Asherah. Now it was *dark* dark, and the tallow lamp was blown out while the darkness was thick, hungry, and everywhere.

There was no moon tonight, had been no moon for three nights now, and the sky outside the window was full of dark angry clouds that swirled and boomed and sent hot winds snarling around the sleeping room to keep the darkness awake. There was no moon, and a storm was coming, so tonight was the very worst kind of night.

And Geula had fallen asleep.

She'd fallen asleep for a long time, long enough for Immi and Abbi to finish talking and come to bed, long enough for Asherah to wake up, and long enough for the darkness to grow thick and hungry around her. Geula could feel it now, the waiting, silent darkness hovering over her bed, getting ready to swallow her whole. *I'm awake now*, Geula whispered to herself, careful not to let any sound get past her lips. *I'm awake now, and it can't eat me when I'm watching it.*

She was so tired. And her eyes burned while holding them open. She needed to blink just once.

If I'm awake, Geula wondered—but it was hard to wonder for long when she was so sleepy—*and it's* dark *dark in the sleeping room, then how am I seeing Asherah?*

#

How can I see Asherah?

She sat up on her mat, suddenly wide awake and full of terror, whipping her head around in the darkness and trying to see something—anything—except black.

How can I see Asherah? It's dark and the alcove is always dark first, and the altar is dark, and how can I see Asherah?

"The same way," Asherah murmured in the darkness beside her, "that I can always see you, Geula."

Geula felt the pee flowing out of her, hot and stinking, soaking her thighs and her mat. Immi would whip her for it tomorrow—if there was a tomorrow—but Asherah was today, right now, and she was realer than a hundred thousand lots of whippings. Asherah was right there, and she was big, and she was talking to Geula. *It is probably rude to pee yourself in front of a goddess*, Geula thought, and she felt her cheeks growing hot like the puddle of wet on her mat.

"Hush," Asherah whispered, and Geula felt a cool hand touch her face. "I won't hurt you."

She laughed. Her breath smelled like lilies and that was all right because she couldn't stay scared of someone who laughed like that. Not even in the darkness, she couldn't fear Asherah.

Geula understood that now. There was nothing to be afraid of.

"Come with me," Asherah laughed. Geula stood, but her legs were wet and dripping. She felt her cheeks turning red again, and the darkness rose with her shame. She sat down, back on the wet bed, cowering from the darkness. But Asherah kissed her on the forehead and whispered, "Come, Geula."

Geula stood again.

This time she was light, lighter than wind, and the darkness fell back and cowered from her. It was a wonderful thing to be in the darkness—surrounded by darkness—and to not be afraid at all.

Asherah took Geula's hand, and Geula followed her. Together, they pushed the darkness away, and left shining footprints made of moonlight behind them. Hand in hand, they left the sleeping room, and Abbi and Immi, and the heavy wet frightened lump of fear that had been Geula until Asherah kissed her. Until Asherah made her real.

They left the room and the house and walked out underneath the wild, angry, cloudy sky into the howling angry wind, and Geula felt herself grow heavy with fear again.

"Hush," Asherah said, lifting her face, letting the wind whip her hair. Geula copied her.

The wind blew through her, carrying away the fear, and she closed her eyes and felt the storm in her and around her until there was no room to be afraid, nowhere in her anymore. There was only Geula, and Geula wasn't afraid of anything.

Asherah smiled and Geula opened her eyes. The sky was full of stars. They glittered and danced, hanging beneath the swirling storm clouds, so close that Geula thought she might be able to touch one if she were just a little taller. She stretched out her hands, trying to do just that, and felt the warmth of their light filling her palms, spilling out to wash over her.

"It's beautiful," she whispered, reaching up on her tiptoes, trying to get a little closer.

"Remember this," Asherah said. Her voice was soft and sad.

Geula turned to look, to see why the goddess was unhappy, but she was gone.

"Remember me," came Asherah's voice on the wind. And then the stars began to fall. They fell like diamonds at first, bright and beautiful and glittering with fire inside them, a rain of jewels across the cities. They fell tinkling onto the stone and brick, and then some of them broke open, and the fire inside leapt out of them, bright and hungry, looking for something to eat, something to burn. The fire crawled across the ground, getting closer and closer to Geula until she could feel it biting at her, sharp and fierce and painful.

#

Geula sat up in bed, choking on her screams, opening her eyes.

It was only a dream. She'd fallen asleep and the darkness was going to eat her for falling asleep, but Geula knew now there were worse things than the darkness. There were worse things than being swallowed in your sleep. Geula drew in a gasping breath, and the air was thick and black, and the darkness wasn't darkness, after all. It was something trying to climb down her throat and eat her from the inside and she could still see Asherah. She could see the little alcove and the statue, and the glittering crown all full of fire and starlight, and something slammed through the roof of the sleeping room. Then everything was on fire.

"Abbi! Immi!" Geula screamed into the choking smoke that filled the sleeping room, the smoke that came from the burning stars crashing through the roof, from the corner where they should have been sleeping. She screamed again and again, but nobody answered her. The whole world was full of smoke and fire, and Geula huddled on her sleeping mat while the stars fell all around her. Her eyes stung and her throat burned and there wasn't any air anywhere in the whole world. She couldn't breathe. The fire was in her lungs and all around her.

Geula screamed and reached for Asherah, but the goddess wasn't moving now. There was fire in her screams and fire on her sleeping mats, and Asherah wasn't listening. It had only been a dream.

She tried to run, but the stars were falling around her, shaking the ground, and her feet were melting, and she couldn't move. Geula tried to close her eyes, and tried again, and tried a third time, wishing—praying—for the darkness and the familiar fear to come back, but her eyes wouldn't close. Her feet wouldn't move, and the darkness wouldn't come. It would never come again.

In the alcove, the baked clay cracked and crumbled, and the bronze crown fell, melting to the ground. As it pooled and ran, the screaming stopped.

WARMTH

Kris Varga

Cold. The word shutters over the mind. Cold is the cobbled streets on the brink of winter, resonating with the season appropriately. Cold is the city under a dainty snowfall while fleeting teal sparks reach for the heavens. Cold is the sound of vacancy among Gomorrah, whose electricity has been discontinued via an electromagnetic pulse. Cold is the soul at the brink of survival.

Patrick was cold.

"The Day of Shock," Patrick creatively coined it, left him immobile and incapable of returning to an energy pod to restore his battery. He computed a light chuckle in his thoughts, one that was innocent enough to maintain the positive attitude he was designed to omit. His bio-constructed flesh tingled as his eyes transfixed on snowy open vastness. Patrick had traveled this path many times, but this time he gained a new perspective, catching a glimpse of himself as if a stranger. He computed a silent sigh.

"Soon enough," he speculated, "Evelyn will return."

Evelyn always returned.

#

Four days, two hours, thirty-six minutes and fifty-seven seconds ago, Patrick and Evelyn had passed through the quieter outlets of the city's boundaries: the grasslands, as they were referred to by the people of Gomorrah. Their weekly destination, however routine, pleased Patrick.

Beyond the bubble-shaped buildings and transcendent automobiles, emitting violent screeches to convey each individual's animosity towards another, laid the incandescent fields, preserved for the rare produce proprietors who lived a "simpler life." Twenty-four degrees above the Earth's meeting with the sky rested the sun, whose lackadaisical clock reminded Patrick of the bells that would ring ever so briefly from Divine Intelligence's control tower. The grocery bags in Patrick's hands would only slow down their travels.

"Patrick, slow down! I wanna enjoy the sunset."

"My dear, we must hurry—for time, you see, is dwindling. It is almost the eve."

"Sing me the Clair de Lune." Her eyes smiled their childish embellishment. "Pretty please?"

Patrick halted and glanced cheerfully at the heart of the city, then at the enticing sun, then at Evelyn's purity. Against all odds, Evelyn's smile won out, and she placed her knapsack on the ground and rested cross-legged in the open field as Patrick hummed the tune to his best ability. Even though this was not a part of his programming, Evelyn seemed to enjoy the flawed sound he produced. "Human-like", she would call it.

#

Patrick tried for the sixteen-thousandth and seventy-fourth time to move his finger. Unsuccessful. In the far left he could hear several dogs (five, he confirmed) gnawing at limp flesh. *I pray they are well fed* were the non-verbal hopes of the malnourished Patrick. Despite his mechanical construction and electric operation, his system still operated on the concept of nutrition. At this point, given the circumstances, he calculated his life-expectancy at five hours, sixteen minutes, and ten seconds. "Evelyn will return."

Earnest optimism, as he could convey no other, hovered over his alloyed skull.

Forty-two meters ahead of him emerged two silhouettes from the drifting snowfall. Forty-one meters later, they blocked the open vastness that laid before Patrick. It was the taller wanderer who spoke first.

"Well, what do you know? I reckon we found a working humanoid, Joe."

Joe's beady eyes scanned Patrick, alighting with a malicious grin as his blood-red bandanna slid down his neck. "It does seem that we did, Bert." Joe quickly pushed Patrick's left shoulder, who returned unwillingly to his original positioning. "Looks like this one managed to survive Divine Intelligence's EMP blast."

Patrick's mind was working faster than the rest of his parts. Other humanoids did not survive? He only assumed they were all in a similar predicament, waiting for Divine Intelligence to send out refugees. Patrick was waiting for someone else.

#

"Okay. Now you watch the sunset and, this time, I'll sing for you."

This was a different circumstance. Evelyn had avoided singing ever since her mother had passed. She was renowned for her beautiful voice, one that would stop the angels from their choir, yet she refused to share it with the world anymore. Patrick remained cheerfully calm yet pleaded in appropriate congruence to the situation.

"Evelyn, please, my darling, we must return. As happy as I am for you to wish to sing, I do believe it is of greater importance to return to the city. Father would be most upset with me if he discovered us out in the grasslands at this hour."

"I promise everything will be okay." She rested her graceful hand on Patrick's arm. "Trust me."

Patrick trusted Evelyn more than anyone. He released a computed chuckle, one that was innocent enough to maintain the positive attitude he was designed to omit.

"As I am obedient to your every will, I shall rest for the duration of the song you choose to sing." His mechanical eyes fixated upon hers, creating a fatherly display, one of sincerity, as they released a twinkle to lighten the mood. "But, afterwards, we shall return to the safety of your father's house. Now, if you will …"

#

The two men encircled Patrick with curiosity. Their postures were stiff and alert, taking cat-like strides, as if Patrick were to pounce at any given moment. After three minutes and sixteen seconds of this, the men conversed at ease seven feet behind Patrick, leaving their supply packs within arms distance of Patrick.

"What should we do with him?"

"Strip off his skin and sell the parts. Donnie Whitemark will buy them for a good price."

This seemed most unusual to Patrick, for he had only heard stories of men like this yet never encountered the "scoundrels" personally. At his home, he was confined behind the upper-class walls and only left the premises to accompany Evelyn on their grocery trips. Father refused to give details but reminded them of the men who haunt the nights, committing sinful acts upon the virtuous. What Evelyn learned among her peers was much more graphic: violent attacks of unexplainable means by tormented souls who eat the flesh of other humans and take part in illegal sexual activity while under intoxicating paraphernalia. Humanoids were members of both parties—the virtuous and the sinful.

Suddenly, Patrick was lying on his back with two knives and two matching grins shining in the bleak apparel of midnight. At the angle they placed him, Patrick was able to get his first look at Gomorrah since "The Day of Shock." It was horrific, and it was the first time in his life that Edward's cheeriness was matched.

The wonderfully bright city, one that radiated a glow that paired the tranquil sensitivity of Evelyn's blue eyes, was of rubble and darkness, with only a few remaining sparks and embers to ignite the reminder of the Heaven-to-Hell which came to be. Only Divine Intelligence's tower stood erect, as it was the only building made of natural concrete instead of bio-manufactured polyester, similar to the making of

Edward's skin.

The two knives created their incision, sliding over the stomach and across the chest. Patrick could feel the searing pain of open flesh to the ice of dainty snow laying in him like a fragrant dream. *No, a nightmare!* screamed Patrick's thoughts. Where was his Evelyn?

#

The sliding of the reassuring sun called the chimes at their precise daily time. Patrick faced the sunset and drifted his mind away from calculations, pouring his thoughts to the beauty of the whispering wind as Evelyn began her melody from behind. At first, Patrick did not recognize the tune, only to realize it was a lullaby Mother would sing to Evelyn at night when she feared the monitors that recorded the vandals outside the perimeters. The words, this time, were changed:

"Call me, oh angel, with strings of your harp
guided by wings in the dawn of the dark
if only my prayers were enough
to induce my love, for you, my love.
Call me, oh angel, with kings of the heart
silent dreams will breathe your restart
if only my prayers were enough
to protect my love of you, my love.
Carry me, oh angel, beyond the tall walls
I am in need of the leave, you may fall
to your knees, but try to be tough
my love, be free, my one true love."

A single tear fell down Patrick's cheek, glistening in the frozen sun. Never had he cried before nor knew it was even something he was capable of conveying. As his breaths heavily inhaled and exhaled, a faint zapping sound released in the background. Evelyn kissed Patrick passionately on the cheek—it seemed to last forever—and whispered "goodbye."

The shuffle of light footsteps stretched farther and farther away.

Patrick was accustomed to Evelyn running off and Patrick having to chase her. He would catch her; they would laugh and return home. Patrick tried to turn and play the game once again but found himself incapable of doing so. It was as if he had forgotten how to move. "Evelyn?" he tried to speak, but not a single sound was muttered. He tried several more times, and several more times after that. And several more after that.

#

The pain was unbearable. Screams were fighting their way through inconceivable odds and forming something more than thoughts.

"Look, Joe. This here is real aluminum alloy. We're rich. Filthy rich!"

Evelyn was not returning. If she were hiding in the bushes, as she always had, she would have run out to save him. She would have attacked the men with all the power she could muster. And here he was, alone, with no one to help him.

Patrick was angry. Furious, even, at Evelyn for abandoning him, furious at the evil of men whose selfishness was destroying him, furious at Divine Intelligence for leaving him so helpless and vulnerable, furious at his creator for designing him to the falsity of his beliefs. Most of all, he was furious at himself. For not once in his life had he ever stabbed a man.

The blood streamed from Joe's stomach, and his beady eyes turned into a ghastly horror. Another flash of pain breached Patrick's side as Bert stuck in his knife and stood in defense. Patrick removed the knife and threw it directly into Bert's elongated forehead, causing him to fall instantly to his death.

"How the hell—?" Joe sputtered as he shuffled on the ground, holding his wound.

Patrick hovered over Joe, the blood-soaked knife dripping with rage. Patrick glanced over his own open body, removed Bert's coat, and covered himself. Despite his wounds, his body was at full capacity. Patrick grabbed Joe's throat and held the knife to the esophagus.

"Where is Evelyn?" he growled.

"Who the fuck is Evelyn?" Bert yelped.

Patrick cut Bert's face. Bert howled in agony. The man was clearly uninformed in this matter, so Patrick recalculated his next question.

"What happened to me?"

"There ... there was an EMP," Bert slurred the words with blood trickling from his mouth. "Divine Intelligence ... it destroyed the city ... corrupt ... it said ... humans were corrupt."

"My people and I were destroyed because your people were too corrupt?"

Bert coughed and Patrick tossed him aside like a useless toy. Why would Divine Intelligence punish him for their mistakes? Had Evelyn known this would happen? Patrick demanded answers.

"You can't leave me here to die. It's immoral!"

Patrick computed a sneer and walked towards the last standing city building.

Smoldering smoke rose towards the heavens, complementing the teal sparks and rash embers as a blend of all divinity. The tower remained unscathed, informing Patrick that this was the only place a survivor could remain in the city. Using his aluminum alloy hand, he punched through the door and admitted himself.

The tower's interior was of a traditional, ancient style. It represented everything the city was not: conservative, disciplined, and intact. One could wonder at the irony of a modern city being controlled by a building of this nature. Light began to shine in Patrick's eyes, both metaphorically and physically, as a single individual approached him.

"Hello. I am Divine Intelligence."

The man resembled a human, but what was missing was a single flaw on the body. In fact, it looked neither man nor woman and showed no sign of an actual age. A single white cloak covered the body.

Patrick fumed and immediately attacked the figure with his barbaric knife. The figure defended itself with ease.

"Patrick, I'm disappointed in you." The figure glided over a throne-like chair and placed itself on it. "I'm sure you have questions in regard to the city's current predicaments."

"Where's Evelyn?" Patrick demanded. His voice was hoarse, and he lost all sense of manners.

Divine Intelligence smiled. "I created humanoids in the image of myself. I sought to better the world with their presence, but there were flaws. Some turned to the side of sin, taking advantage of the concept of free will and destroying all things pure. Others, like yourself, were too ignorant, took no initiative, and fell to a life of servitude. This comfort made you weak and useless."

Patrick grimaced. After his body returned to life, he expected his warmth to return, as well. He had never felt colder.

"So, you see, I set off the EMP, purging the city from my creation. The upper-class were notified ahead of time and the rest were left to their own demise. Any who tried to take a humanoid with them forfeited the law and were sentenced to death."

Divine Intelligence stood at this and pensively stared out the window for a moment. Then, it turned and stared at Patrick, who was preparing his next attack.

"WHERE IS EVELYN?"

"Please, set yourself at ease. You come off as a fool. To continue, all humanoids were to immediately deactivate, but you managed to hang on to life. Barely." Divine Intelligence took a few steps forward. "You see, the distance from the tower put you just far enough to keep you stable. Immobile, but stable."

Before Patrick could shout again, Divine Intelligence raised a hand.

"Very well. I shall show you what you wish to see."

A monitor appeared, the same kind that used to show the vandals outside the perimeters of the wall. It was of the woods, the one that connected to the grasslands, and carefully wandering through the woods were a group of humans. They seemed to be moving in formation, each handling a responsibility in the function of the group. Amid the pack was—

"Evelyn!"

As if she heard Patrick, her head turned and glanced around. She took a deep breath then returned to her group.

"As you can see, she is quite well, and in very good hands. These humans have formed a connection in these dire circumstances, one based on the principles of safety, survival, and morality. It is quite remarkable."

This information ran through Patrick like rain through a ditch. *She is alive*, he thought. *That's all that matters.*

Patrick glanced at Divine Intelligence, who waited for a response.

"So, what happens next?" Patrick asked.

"Well, let me introduce you to someone very special. Follow me this way."

Patrick followed, begrudgingly. They walked up a marble staircase and into an elegant room lined with silk linen and a well-crafted tapestry. In the far-right corner sat a beautiful woman, who kept silent upon their entrance. Divine Intelligence spoke first.

"This is Julia," it said, waving a hand towards the woman.

"Hello," spoke the woman with an inviting smile. Julia stood and maneuvered gracefully to Patrick, nodding politely. Patrick glanced back and forth from Julia to Divine Intelligence with curiosity.

"Julia," said Divine Intelligence, "is just like you, Patrick. A humanoid survivor. Together, I shall use the two of you to create the perfect being. Between the three of us, we shall find a cure for the plague of humanity."

Patrick was dizzy with confusion. He began to ask questions, using the word "why" at the beginning of each one, but he found that there were no conceivable answers. He swayed back and forth until he felt a soft hand on his shoulder.

"It's okay, my love," the gentle voice of Julia soothed him, "everything will be okay."

With that, Julia took Patrick by the hand, and they followed Divine Intelligence to the top of the tower where an energy pod recharged their batteries.

Patrick felt warm.

THE SCENT OF SIN AND PUNISHMENT

J.P. Cianci

I drink deeply from my half-filled chalice, admiring the way the indelibly perfect, golden idol of Molech reflects the sunlight. I raise my goblet to Molech, my jewel-encrusted cup catching the brilliant rays of the sun, then I take another insatiable drink. I turn around to refill my cup when gentle fingertips run up and down my back.

"Adaron, how would you like to receive Molech's blessing?" Sahar whispers seductively.

I smile, reveling in her touch, and close my eyes. I imagine all the delicious ways in which her body could satisfy the pressing fleshly urges her contact has aroused. "I would love to receive Molech's blessing, but I cannot afford such a sanction," I say, opening my eyes. I cup the temple prostitute's breast and forcefully bring her in for a kiss.

She smacks me, but I laugh and grab her wrist.

"Come now, Sahar. I worship in here every day. I'm entirely devoted. Are you sure Molech wouldn't want to bless a follower such as myself?"

"If you need money to afford his blessing, I know someone who would pay handsomely for the company of your daughter," Sahar suggests.

I smack her quick and hard across the face, holding a finger to her—warning her—but I say nothing.

She slinks off to find another, no doubt richer, follower to seduce.

Incense wafts from silver plates beneath the idol and I try to forget Sahar and her remarks. I don't need to pay to satisfy my desires. Many women, and even men, are happily drawn in by my sexual prowess.

I walk drunkenly back to the idol that is gloriously exposed to the sun by the open rooftop of the temple and fall to my knees in prayer. I slur my pleas and wishes for a few moments before my head bobs heavily from the wine. After an hour, I close my eyes to rest at the foot of Molech, basking in the afternoon sun.

"It's too early to be this dark," someone remarks a few minutes later.

"Quiet!" I bark. My eyes are still closed, but I do notice the almost imperceptible shift in light behind my eyelids. "It's merely clouds passing in the sky."

"What is that? A sandstorm?" someone else asks. The presence of a crowd gathering around me causes me to finally open my eyes.

"Gawk outside! Do not waste Molech's temple for slack-jawed gaping!" I yell, but no one listens. I raise my head to the sky, which is shrouded in darkness. Plumes of smoke billow downward in waves, obscuring the sun.

"Sandstorms don't move like that," I say, shifting uneasily. People murmur excitedly all around me.

"It's all right! I see light!"

"Yes! I see it too! It looks like the sun is coming toward us!"

"That's not light, that's fire! Run!"

"No! This is a sacred temple. We are safe here," I assure them, but people take off to the streets. I kneel a few feet back from Molech and begin fervently praying. As the smoke surges closer, I cover my mouth and nose in disgust, but only for a moment. A ball of fire collides directly with my sacred idol. A stream of melted gold sprays in my direction, blinding me in one eye and cooling rapidly to my skin so that it's encased in a painful, golden mask.

I moan in agony, turning to flee. "Oh Molech, Oh Molech. Why? *Why?*" I'm almost to the entrance of the temple when it collapses on top of me.

#

"Hey! Hey!"

My eyes flutter open.

"I knew you were alive. I could hear you breathing," a man says, lying across from me in the ruins of the temple. His face is charred, and his left limb is pinched beneath a stone slab.

My eyes tear from my own pain.

"You've been out for three days," he says. "I'm Jaban."

"Adaron," I gasp.

"I can't move, Adaron. It looks like you might be able to. If you can, you can go for help, yes? Can you find help and save me?" he asks.

I lay my head weakly on the ground. I'm confined to my belly, and this small exertion of energy from lifting my head—now heavy with gold—taxes me.

"Wake up, you fool! Can you move?" he hisses.

I'm in too much pain to be upset. I can't feel or move my legs, but my face pulses in pain. I glance at my hands with my one good eye. They're the only part of me that I can move freely, and they are scorched but functional.

"I can't move my legs," I say, simply.

"Argh! You haven't tried! You could save me—us!"

I lay my head back down. All I want to do is sleep to escape the pain.

What feels like hours later, pebbles clink against my golden face plate. I open my eyes to darkness.

"Adaron! Can you feel your legs now?" Jaban asks.

I sigh, trying to wriggle them.

"No—"

"Shh! Wait! Do you hear that?" he interrupts.

I strain my ears, "Yes, I hear voices!"

"Here! We're here!" Jaban cries.

"We're here!" I echo.

Rapid footsteps approach us, but their full forms are obscured in the plumes of smoke that still linger. I can't see three feet above me.

"No! What are you doing?" I cry as a man bends down and grasps at the golden mask that is now a part of my body. "No! Please! *Please!*"

"This one has a face of gold. Come help me pry it off!" the man yells.

Two more men appear, and the three of them grab hold, ignoring my shrieks of agony. I puff in and out quickly, trying to withstand the pain. When that doesn't work, I try to hold my breath, but the pain is too much. "*No! Stop!*"

The sickening rip of skin and the nauseous heat of my pain cause me to vomit. The men hoot in victory and leave us.

"If you had tried to escape like I suggested earlier, this would not have happened to you," Jaban says cruelly.

"Why did you not say anything?" I cry, bringing a shaky hand to my damaged and raw face.

"You are not a friend to me," he says.

I try to hold onto consciousness, but my pain forces me to sleep. Before I close my eyes, I note the broken, gold pieces of Molech that the robbers must not have seen because of the smoke. I cry pitifully at the unfairness until I drift off.

#

"This is a punishment from Lot's God. Lot knew, but he fled. He left them to their rightful fate!" a woman proclaims.

"Ten. They said if ten righteous people lived within these walls they could have been saved," another says. "How could there not have been ten?" she questions, but there is no pity in her voice.

They hurry past me, but I don't bother asking for help. I know better now.

So, Lot's God did this. How could his God do such a thing? And how am I not righteous? I lived like all the others.

I lick my chapped lips. "Jaban?"

"What?"

"How long have I been out this time?" I ask.

"Two more days. You will die here, no doubt," he predicts.

"Yes, well, when you lift that stone slab that pinches your left limb, I'll be sure to marvel at your godlike strength that could have saved me when you leave me here to die," I say.

"You idiot! I can't feel my arm!"

"And I can't feel my legs as I've told you before!"

I sigh and let a few moments pass. He is my only link. "What happened to Sodom?" I question.

"The same thing that happened to Gomorrah. Lot's God proclaimed that these two cities were full of sinners, and we were meant to feel his wrath. Wanderers from Zoar have been walking the streets to see for themselves. They were the only city that was spared."

"They wouldn't help you?" I question.

"They are afraid of God's wrath. They believe we are all meant to perish," he says, sounding weary. "Go back to sleep. You bore me, and this talk is meaningless. I need to save my energy."

I'm silent after that, and it lasts through the next two days. I stay awake the entire time, listening as the wanderers comment and take in God's wrath. When the sun rises and peaks through the smoke on the second day of reflection, I know it will be my last.

I weakly lift my head. The acrid, foul smoke suffocates, but it won't kill me. I wheeze and lay my head back down, closing my eyes. I gasp, trying to take deep breaths, but every breath, though it may prolong my life, repulses my senses.

A grunt makes me raise my head. Jaban feebly reaches for the bits of gold that remain, and I laugh, delirious.

"What do you plan on doing with the gold? And how could you spend it?" I ask.

He ignores me, keeping to silence and palming the gold in his only remaining hand.

A baby cries in the distance, and I stiffen with sadness. When the crying persists, I break into sobs, my delirium gone. In all this time, I had not given a single thought to my only child—only to my own fate.

"Anna," I whisper, thinking now only of my three-year-old daughter. I had left her with our neighbors so I could worship. What of her now? Had she survived?

I remember what the woman had said about the righteous. How could my Anna not be righteous? How could she be forsaken? And how short was our number? The woman said that only ten righteous souls were needed to save Sodom and Gomorrah. Was it only Anna? Or not even Anna? Will she pay for my many sins?

"Oh, Anna! Are you eternally lost? Have I damned you?" I weep.

Were there nine? If I had accepted Anna's mother's death and rejoiced in her eternal life, instead of turning away from the faith and blaming God, would I have saved Anna? Would I have made ten?

I clutch at the gravel.

"Hello? Is anyone alive here?" a soft voice asks.

I'm silent as tentative steps draw closer.

"Mother, why do we linger here? It's unsafe."

"The wicked have been punished. Those who still cling to life might still be saved," she answers.

"Here. I am here," I croak, assured of their intentions

"What is your name?" the woman asks, bending to give me water.

"Adaron," I answer.

She assesses my body and furrows her brow. "I can't get you out, but we will pray over you before you die, imploring God to save you," she says, knowing—as I know—that death is upon me.

"No, please. My daughter. Can you find my daughter?"

"We should not risk God's wrath by helping this man. Let us go back to Zoar," the daughter says, gripping her mother's arm.

"I can try. I can bring her to you if we find her," the woman says, taking my hand and giving it a squeeze.

"No! I don't want her to see me. She is only three. If I tell you where you might find her, will you see if she is alive? I just want to know that she is alive. I will let you pray over me then."

"We should pray first, and you should, too," the woman insists.

"So that I can be saved, and Anna cannot? No, if Anna is dead … please, can you do this for me? Please?" I beg.

"Well, all right. Tell me where to find this child," she says, her gentle hands moving a lock of my hair out of my eyes.

I give directions and wait in an agonizing eternity, with nothing to do than to recount my sins. I inhale a deep breath, but it chokes me.

Sin and punishment have very distinct smells, I've come to realize, lying in the rubble, dying next to the dead and soon-to-be dead.

I inhale the bitter, foul stench that loiters with the fog. It mixes with the stink of the charred flesh of my own body and the man next to me. It mixes still with the excrement of the dead and trapped. This is the pungent odor of punishment, but there is another odor I detect. It is a similar thread between the smell of sin and the smell of punishment.

It is the metallic scent of blood. Perhaps it is a similarity I'm meant to recognize. A common thread meant for me to reflect upon, as I smell its scent now in punishment. Maybe I'm the only one to pick this out.

For murder was my first sin.

Three years ago, a young man walked late at night down the streets of Zoar where I had been visiting, and I recognized the alluring clink of gold coin against gold coin. I stared lustfully at the man's heavy pouch as he drunkenly made his way down the empty streets. I approached him under the guise of friendliness and asked if I could escort him home. I was careful, even for my first time. He led me to his house, and once inside, I slit his throat and slit the pouch from off his belt. I murdered this innocent creature, one of God's innocent lambs.

I grab one of the gold bits of an idol and hurl it in disgust. The money lasted briefly, and the blood washed off easily, but I could never separate the smell of gold from the smell of blood after that. Strangely now, it seems fitting that I would have to endure the golden mask, only to have it ripped away with flesh and blood: A reminder of my sin.

That is not my only sin. I breathe in the sinful scent of incense from the temple. It still burns from the fiery rainfall. It's thicker than usual, unpleasant now. Did He mean to keep this burning for me? To remember and repent?

How often had I danced merrily with the other citizens of Sodom around our sacred idols? I drank deeply and feasted gluttonously, exulted exuberantly, and revered falsely these now-broken idols. How often had I lusted to fornicate with the temple prostitutes? How foolishly had I believed that I would receive the blessing of the deity they represented? A sin in itself to lust, I now realize, and it had been the gateway that had led me to the last stain on my mortal record.

I cough and splutter, only to inhale the scent of my punishment.

I remember a wedding celebration, one year ago, where a man and his new wife danced sensually in front of the invited crowd. Oh, how I lusted for the wife. The way she danced with him reminded me of the pleasures I once had with my own wife. I never cared to know the man, and I never did, but his wife … his wife I came to know most intimately. It could hardly be my fault that she wavered in her devotion to her husband. She was easily seduced by my desire. She was my sweetest sin. This sin smelled the loveliest, for she smelled of jasmine.

I inhale deeply, thinking of her, but only sniff the putrid excrement of the men around me who have been laid to waste. I shrink in shame for remembering her lustfully still.

I glance at Jaban, but he is unnervingly motionless.

I know now that I'm meant to suffer. Death will come soon, I feel it, but I've come to believe that I'm meant to writhe in pain amidst the rubble. That I'm meant to die in agony for Him—for my sins. Could this be my penance? Will He let it be my penance?

"Adaron?" the woman whispers.

Yes! I'm here!" my voice comes raspy.

She drops to her knees by my side. I gaze up at her hopefully. She smiles gently at me, but her face is lined with pity.

A dry sob wracks my body.

"I'm sorry," the woman replies. "We found the neighbor who struggles to survive, but I'm afraid Anna is gone. Your neighbor gave me this." The woman opens her hand and gives me the bright red ribbon that I used to secure Anna's hair that fateful morning seven days ago.

I weep into the ground, grasping this only vestige of my child.

"It's time to repent of your sins. It's time to pray. There is a chance you may be saved," she urges, pulling her daughter down to the ground next to her.

Their moving lips begin to breathe formulaic words into clasped hands, and my head lolls on the ground. I'm ready to go, but not where these women mercifully hope to send me.

I have heard that God created the Earth, and then on the seventh day he rested. It is the seventh day since His wrath, and this will only mark the beginning of a restless eternity in damnation for me.

"No," I say, reaching up to grab their hands, and then I slowly lower them. "I must wander the fires below with Anna," I say, and I forcefully breathe in a final whiff of the scent of my punishment.

SOLOMON'S LOT

Allen Taylor

Solomon peeked around the corner of Mr. Krauss's General Store. After taking a deep breath, he stepped into the shadow of the clay awning hanging over the door. He was hungry for not having eaten in three days.

Pedestrians bustled through the streets of Sodom from one end of the city to the other. Most were going to or from market. Others were busying themselves with activity to mask their fear or worry of impending doom. Fruit vendors, craftspeople, and various merchants lined the streets with carts. The sounds of buyers and sellers bartering, cutting deals, negotiating, and crafting transactions filled Solomon's ears like a chorus. A part of him felt the stab of envy from the inside out. He had been jobless for a week and therefore had no money for buying goods, food, subsistence. He was tired of begging.

He pushed himself behind a man selling pomegranates and into the door of the store where it was considerably darker without the benefit of the sunshine penetrating the stone walls. He stopped to let his eyes adjust. When he could see the divisions of aisles, he continued, walking through the store to the back where no one could see him.

It, too, was busy. He picked the wrong time of day to take up thievery. But he couldn't deny the pangs of hunger that riveted his flesh from bare foot to brow. He waited for the woman and two children tugging at her arm to round the corner to the next aisle before snatching a small box of dried fruit from a shelf and tucking it into his tunic.

He dilly-dallied a little longer, skipping aisles to find one without hustling buyers aggressively pursuing their needs. It proved a much more difficult task than finding items to snatch and stow.

After a half hour of trying to remain anonymous, he gave up and snuck past the merchants calculating their sales and outside into the street again, then around the store's corner. He sat on a ledge protruding from the outside wall of the store and glanced both ways down the street before pulling a goatskin full of fig juice from his tunic followed by the box of dried fruit and a small loaf of bread.

It wasn't long before a boy—he couldn't have been older than twelve or fourteen—ran past, then just as quickly returned again to Solomon, standing before the old vagrant and looking pensively as if waiting to speak. The boy waited until Solomon looked up from his goodies before talking.

"Have you heard the news, sir?"

Solomon felt like being rude and sniping at the boy, but he didn't want to draw attention to himself. "Wha' news?"

The boy coughed, covering his mouth with his fist, and spat on the street. When he spoke again, his voice cracked. But he managed to force himself to spill his proclamation.

"Ol' Sal's going to blow any day now, what they say. All the peoples are running for cover, buying up their needs afore it gets too bad. Could destroy the city."

Solomon didn't respond. Instead, he shoved a piece of bread into his face and growled. The boy, satisfied he had delivered the message, turned and ran away as Solomon lifted the goatskin to his lips and sucked from its horn. He finished his makeshift meal, aware of its lack, and shuffled his feet in the dirt that made up the city street. As he wondered what to do next, he watched the people scatter like ants across the city square, some running in that direction and many others pushing themselves in the opposite. He considered whether the boy's warning should be taken seriously. Ol' Sal, he knew—all city residents knew—was the tall mountain of rock situated at the edge of the sea on the outskirts of Sodom. Legend had it the mountain had exploded, shooting hot fire and rock sometime in the distant past, though it had been many years since it had even so much as rumbled. No one alive had ever witnessed it. As far as Solomon knew, it was nothing more than legend. But today, it would be more than that.

Something shattered on the street. Solomon sat unfazed, finishing the last morsel of bread he held in his hand. Then he followed that with a final swallow of juice before tossing the packet to the ground.

Another splatter.

It looked like fire. He thought he must be hallucinating. Fire doesn't fall from the sky.

Then it happened again. A rock hit the street and broke into little pieces, each of them red hot and smoldering. Suddenly, people started running, and he heard screams of terror. Hysteria. People were tripping over themselves and each other. A man running by tumbled face forward into the street right in front of Solomon and yelped on his way to pounding his face into well-trafficked sand. Solomon jumped to his feet.

The man didn't move. Solomon looked around. No one was coming to save the man. Was he dead?

The stone roof of the store he had been leaning on had sheltered Solomon enough from the falling rocks that he didn't worry. A couple of balls of fire hit the roof and bounced off, landing in the street next to the dead man. His clothes caught fire and Solomon looked up at the sky for a break. When he thought he could get away with it, he jumped into the street and felt the man's clothes for something to steal. He found a pouch with coins in it and a couple of pieces of jewelry. He took them. Before leaping back to the side of the building, he yanked the broach off the man's neck and got out of the way of a careening rock just in time. A woman fell beside him, hitting the building and bouncing back into the street. She, too, tumbled over dead. Solomon suddenly felt lucky to be alive.

He wondered how he was going to get home, then he remembered he had no home. He had lost that with his job.

The fiery rain pelted the streets harder. Where before it had been a drizzling hazard of hard rock rain, it had now become a downpour of hot ash, flecks of mountain rock, and smoking brimstone. There was no venturing out into this until it was done. Solomon watched a few more people fall—old men, older ladies, young children and their moms and dads, and even a few animals—then he pressed his back against the store wall and slithered his way around the corner and through the door. It was wall-to-wall huddling shoppers and merchants in there. He barely squeezed through before the store owner, Mr. Krauss, pushed the stone door closed and locked it from the inside.

"No one's going out and no one's coming in. We're closed," he said as he turned and faced the crowd behind him. A crescendo of cheers rose from the sweaty throng of citizens trying their best to tolerate being so close to each other.

A woman at the back of the pack yelled, "What's going on? I've got to get back home before the husband finds me gone!"

"You're not going anywhere, *Wardatu*. It's raining fire out there."

Solomon heard the gruff voice of a man, but he couldn't tell where the voice had come from. It wasn't the store owner. It was someone in the middle of the crowd. A voice from a faceless stranger locked in the same sweatbox as everyone else. Another man argued back, expressing a heartfelt regret that he was being held hostage against his will.

"You're not a hostage, idiot!" Another voice chimed in. "It's deadly out there. Ol' Sal done erupted."

"Poo, Ol' Sal!"

Solomon listened to the voices argue. Some of them took the side of the lady wanting out and the others reiterated the danger lurking out there. Then the crowd began to push and sway. Forward, back, side to side. Solomon pushed his way toward the back of the store, sometimes against the sway and other times making himself a part of it enough that he could propel himself through shoulders and elbows like a fish gliding through water. By the time he reached the back of the store he was soaked with sweat.

"Calm down!" The voice of Mr. Krauss rang over the noise of the crowd. "Calm it, please!"

No one listened. The crowd grew more persuasive in its push toward the door. Before Solomon knew what had happened, the roof caved in the middle of the store. Stone began to crumble and fall onto the heads of men and women, even some of the children. Screams rang out from the front of the store and people pushed toward the corners to get away from the falling rock and the fire that followed. Solomon managed to slip through an open doorway in the back of the store, into Mr. Krauss's vacant office.

Screams filled the store as the crowd pushed. Some pushed to the front of the store toward the door. Others pushed to the sides. Aisles full of foods tumbled forward or back, falling on screaming, petrified citizens of Sodom, injuring or killing them. The roof caved in just enough for missiles of fiery rock to slither between the cracks and land on the store floor or land on a patron and set them aflame. Terrorized citizens filed into the back room with Solomon as he pondered escape through a window in the stone wall.

It seemed as if that room might have been the safest place in the city until panic-stricken Sodomites fled into it. It filled so fast with warm bodies that Solomon hardly knew what to do. He peered through the window to see if he could catch a break in the falling fires of stony rain.

He considered making a run for it, jumping through the window, and taking his chances in the pellets of brimstone ransacking the city. He was about to leap when he heard a voice.

"No! Don't jump. Please."

He turned to see a young woman holding a baby. A girl of not more than fifteen stood beside the desk, tears streaming down her face, looking at Solomon with a sullen, fearful gaze. His heart nearly fell through his stomach. For a moment, he was stricken with guilt over the crimes he had committed. He fought to hold the tears that wanted to fall from his own eyes. In the girl's eyes he could see a reflection of his own fear mingling with hers.

"I've got to go," he said in a guttural whisper. "I can't stay here with—these people."

She knew what he meant. *These people* meant the dying ones. No one would survive this calamity. They both knew it.

"Take me with you," the young mother pleaded.

A fatherly compassion overcame Solomon as he considered the girl's offer. At one hundred and twenty years, he had seen a lot of frightened young women. This one carried a baby, a newborn still in swaddling clothes. Though he could not see its face, Solomon imagined the baby as beautiful as its mother. His wife and eighteen children were miles away in Zoar. His mind drifted to them. How long had it been since he'd seen them? Too long. And now, he thought, he must make his way back to them. He must escape Sodom and go home. He would have to move fast. He couldn't move fast dragging a woman and a child behind like anchors.

"There's an overhang," he said. "Hand me the baby and step through the window. Stay under the overhang."

She did as he commanded. As she slid through the window to the other side of the stone wall and forced herself to stand with her back to the stone to keep away from the falling rock, Solomon lifted a finger to the blanket covering the baby's face. He wanted just one look at the face of the life he would save that day. He pulled the soft wool down below its lips and chin and blinked in shock. Above the infant's lips were a set of tentacles waving at him through the thickening air. Three inches of solid flesh, each of them clamoring for a touch. Below the tentacles, at the corners of the baby's mouth, were a couple of pincers. They looked like they could do some damage. Quickly, he covered the baby's mouth with the blanket and handed it to the woman on the other side of the window.

He had to force himself to climb through. He wanted to run, but there was nowhere to run. He had seen those tentacles. He had seen those pincers. On another being, a not-so-pleasant one. He knew the source of that evil. It was not a creature he wanted to save.

A glance back through the window to the Sodomites filtering into the store owner's office made him rush away. It was run or go back to the crowd. He grabbed the woman's hand and pulled her along the store wall while keeping an eye on the fiery rain to see if there was any chance of it letting up. One man noticed them making their getaway and ran toward the window. He yelled after them as they made their way along the stone wall toward the back corner of the store, careful to remain under the roof hanging over the edge of the building, protecting them from the burning flames falling from the sky. It wouldn't be long, Solomon thought, before the streets were full of people again.

When they reached the corner of the building, Solomon surveyed the street crossing. The rain was falling harder and faster than ever. But he knew they had to try to cross. If they were to ever leave the city, it was the only way. He took the baby off the woman's hands.

"Follow me!"

He darted across the street, dodging the falling rain. Several times he barely escaped being hit. The woman pushed herself beside him, competing to get to the building across the street before he did. When they made it safely across, they stopped, secured their breaths, and waited. Solomon knew they were going to have to take it slow. An old lady crumpled to the ground in the street in front of them and burst into flames. The young mother he was protecting screamed. Solomon huddled over the baby to keep it from hearing its mother.

Solomon grabbed the young woman's hand and pulled her around the building to the other side. The view of the street was no better there than anywhere else. People dying, crying, and getting pummeled to death by sulfurous hail.

"We have a quarter mile to the city gate," Solomon yelled into the woman's ear. "Think you can make it?"

She assured him she could.

He huddled the baby close to his chest and sprinted across the street to the next building. The woman followed. For three blocks they carried out this routine, rounding a building and sprinting across the street. Solomon led the way, cresting the baby in his arms each time as its mother followed, half the time in tears. Finally, they were within eyesight of the city gate. Outside, Solomon wondered if they would be safe from the bullets of fire falling out of the heavens.

"Look! There it is, there it is." The woman was giddy with excitement at the sight of the city gate.

"Yes, we're almost there," Solomon said. "Follow me one more time. We'll dodge the rain to the gate and exit the city. Our best hope is to make our way to Zoar."

The woman agreed. Solomon took off at a run. She followed.

Solomon zigzagged to keep from being hit by rain. He focused his eyes on the city gate, hoping against all hope to make it safely without being hit by the fire falling from above. His heart pumped faster and faster as his spirit filled with glee with each step, closer and closer to salvation. Then he felt something. A nick on his shoulder. A stab. A pinch.

The baby's blanket had fallen to the ground in the hustle from one end of the city to the other. The jostling kept the baby awake, and whether intentional or accidental, Solomon didn't know, but the baby had managed to sting him with its pincers. It startled him and he dropped the baby on his own slow-motion tumble to the surface of the sandy road. The woman leapt over him and tripped, falling to the ground and landing on a knee.

The baby cried. Lying on its face with its rear in the air, it tried to stabilize its body and fell sideways onto its ribs then rolled onto its back just in time to catch a ball of fire in its mouth.

The woman lunged.

"Noooooooooh!" She cried. "My baby! My God, Lazareth. Oh, Lazareth! Lazareth!"

Her tears fell harder than the sulfur rain from the sky. She fell at the baby's side as Solomon pushed himself to his feet and grabbed the woman by the arm. She resisted. He picked her up and threw her over his shoulder. He had committed himself to saving her, and he would. Her body fell limp, helpless to have seen the deadly end of her only child.

Solomon pushed himself toward the city gate. Step after step, heartbeat after heartbeat, he pushed until he was there. When he finally arrived, he ducked into a cubby hole inside the arch where the city guard—who wasn't there—usually stood. The city wall around Sodom took its hits, fire and rock pummeling it from above, setting some of its guard shacks on fire and sending the guards to their deaths below. Solomon slipped into the guard space and sat in the chair that occupied it, holding the woman close to his breast, allowing her the full benefit of his shoulder as she emptied herself of every tear.

The rain continued to fall for hours. Solomon had no idea how long. Eventually, the woman in his arms stopped crying and fell asleep. Darkness came and went. As the sun rose, the sky turned bright blue, showing a promise Solomon had not felt since before the storm. It was the most beautiful morning he had seen in a long time.

He stepped out of the guard stand and stood in the center of the city gate's arch, looking back at the city in shambles. All he could see were buildings crumpled to the ground and bodies everywhere. Most of them had charred beyond recognition, but many of them were simply dead bodies that would soon begin to rot in the heat of the sun and would attract scavengers from both the air and the ground. There was no time to waste and no reason to stay.

The woman stepped out of the guard stand and joined him. She took a step toward the city and Solomon grabbed her arm. He shook his head, signaling that she did not want to go back.

"We must move on," he said.

He could see in her eyes that she did not want that, but she agreed. Their fingers locked. Solomon took her hand and squeezed, trying to comfort her with the strength of his hands. She didn't respond.

"I will protect you all the rest of my days," he said. "I will take you under my roof and you will be my family."

The woman cast her gaze to the ground. She did not want to think about being someone's family. Solomon saw it in her body. She did not want to think about the future, but it would come soon enough and all they would have is memories. The memories of Sodom would fill their hearts and minds forever. Solomon knew it. The woman holding his hand knew it, too.

Solomon turned and pulled her with him. As they exited the city, in the far-off distance, Solomon caught sight the *Maskim Xul.* An army of them. What Ol' Sal didn't do to Sodom, Solomon knew they would. They would destroy what was left of the carnage and wipe it away from the earth. They would asphyxiate any survivors with their tentacles that stretched six feet out from the tops of their lips, which were strong enough to grip a man and squeeze him until his guts spilled out. The dead would become a meal for them. Solomon had seen them feed upon carrion and use the pincers at the corners of their mouths to pick apart the dead flesh of travelers in the desert between the cities of the plain. Now they were coming for Sodom. It was time to move.

"What's your name?" he asked, pulling the woman out of Sodom away from the marching destroyers he hoped she didn't see.

THE REMORSE OF THE INCORPOREUM

AmyBeth Inverness

The rush is disorienting. The loneliness is unbearable. The Word has cast us out. I don't know why. One moment, I was in The Garden at The Beginning, and then …

Here.

I don't fit in Jeremiah. I'm not the only incorporeum who has found this host. We wrestle. We gasp …

Jeremiah suffers.

I grab my other and flee, forward to other hosts.

"Why am I so tired?" Juno asks me.

I smile. "For the best of reasons, my love." Our hosts are in that in-between state, not quite awake, but not quite asleep. This is the safe place. This is the happy place.

Juno can't accept being safe. Juno can't accept being happy.

He leaves, and I follow.

\#

"Mars!" Adam squealed. It came out as more of a "Maaa!" sound ending with something of a growl.

"There, there." Nanny said, going to the small boy. She scooped him up, shivering as she did so. "Oh, goodness, this corner by the window is always cold. Come here with Nanny and I'll read you a book."

Adam pointed at the corner where the cold spot was. "Juno!" he declared happily.

"Juno?" asked Nanny.

"Just Juno," said Adam, snuggling in for story time.

Adam loved story time. Sometimes Mars told him stories when he was all alone, but stories were much better from Nanny. Nanny was warm and soft and always spoke sweetly to him, even when he couldn't find the words he needed.

Nanny rocked, and Adam listened. He was a good boy. He didn't interrupt, even when the colors in the pictures were too bright.

When the story was over, Nanny closed the book and rocked him. The rocking always helped.

"Nah nah?" Adam asked.

"Mmm hmm sweetling?" Nanny answered.

"Why Juno sad?"

"Who's Juno?" Nanny asked.

Adam pointed at the corner by the window.

"Juno miss Kristophe," Adam said, placing his chubby little hands on Nanny's cheeks, hoping she would explain everything to him. Juno was always sad. Mars tried to cheer him up, but nothing ever worked. No story had a happy enough ending to make Juno come out of his corner.

Mars stayed with Adam. Mars was always with Adam, though

sometimes he was quiet. Adam had been the one to give Mars and Juno their names; they tried to claim they were nameless, but Adam would have none of it. Juno grumbled, but Mars laughed, thinking it was only right that a boy named Adam should name them, since the man named Adam had neglected to do so.

Nanny stopped rocking. Her face looked different. Adam couldn't tell if it was a good expression or a bad expression, but he was alarmed that she had stopped rocking. Adam needed to rock. Adam needed to be held. "What did you say, sweetling?" Nanny asked.

"Juno … misses … Kristophe?" Adam wondered if he had the name right. Mars told him stories about Kristophe, and how much Juno loved him, but Kristophe died. "Kristophe died," Adam said, hoping this simple fact would help Nanny figure out what he wanted to know.

"Adam," Nanny said, pushing him off her lap and setting him on the floor. "How do you know about Kristophe?"

Adam swallowed. Something wasn't right. Why wasn't Nanny holding him? Why wasn't she rocking him? Wasn't it time for his nap? "Mah toll me," he explained.

"Your mother told you?" Nanny asked.

Of course, his mother hadn't told him. Adam hadn't seen his mother for weeks, other than outside his window. "No Mama!" Adam declared, trying his very best to be clear. "Mar-zzz." The 'z' sound was fun to make. Adam smiled brightly. He wanted Nanny to smile back.

Nanny wasn't smiling. She wasn't even touching him anymore. She was backing away from him, towards the door. "You … do you see Kristophe? Here?" Nanny asked. Her hand was on the doorknob.

"No," Adam said, worrying. Was Nanny leaving? Did he do something wrong? "Kristophe died."

"Oh. Oh no." Nanny said, slipping out the door before he could follow. "You take your nap now!" she yelled from the stairs.

Adam wailed, his tiny fists pounding on the door. He rattled the knob, but it was locked. It was always locked.

Mars started singing to him, softly, soothingly, and soon, Adam calmed down. The tears still flowed. He was tired, but he couldn't sleep without Nanny rocking him.

A noise from outside caught his attention. Adam stood on his little stool so he could see out the window. His father's carriage had pulled up. His brothers and sisters were pouring out of the house, running to see if he brought them anything from the city. He started handing out little boxes to each of them until they went into the house and Adam couldn't see them anymore.

"Hi, Dada!" Adam said enthusiastically. His father used to look up at the window when he came home. He used to wave, but not anymore.

Adam went to his bed and lay between the sheets, staring at the door. Maybe Dada would come upstairs and bring him a little box from the city. Maybe Nanny would come back and rock him to sleep.

They didn't.

Mars cooed, and sang, and comforted him, while still trying to comfort the inconsolable Juno in the corner. Adam held out as long as he could. If he was just quiet, if he was just still, maybe someone would come.

Sleep took him long before anyone came to see him again.

#

"Kristophe?" Charles whispered. He wasn't sure if the young man was awake or not.

A cough sounded from the bed by the window. "It's all right, Kristophe. I'm here," Charles said. He took the rag off Kristophe's forehead and exchanged it for another. Charles' old, wrinkled hands shook. He hoped this wouldn't be the end. Charles had finally convinced Kristophe's mother to go to bed just a few hours ago. She didn't want to leave her son's side. Kristophe had been fighting the sickness for months now. His parents were exhausted. His mother had even stopped speculating about which young debutantes might catch her son's eye that season, but instead spent all her time in nursing and prayer. Her son had not left her side in the weeks that she had been ill. She blamed herself that he was now suffering even worse than she had.

Charles had been a faithful servant to Kristophe's father for more than twenty years. The arrival of a daughter, then a son, then another daughter had all been celebrated with joy and love. But when Kristophe was born, Charles knew the baby was special. It was like some part of him had been waiting for this particular human to be born. All the family's children looked to him as more of a grandfather than a servant. Kristophe, the youngest, loved him most of all.

#

It is quiet.

Charles doesn't know I'm here. He's not like Adam. But I care for all my Beloveds, whether they know me or not.

Juno cares for his Beloveds too. Sometimes, I think he cares too deeply…

Like with Kristophe. Even long after Kristophe has been reconciled with The Word, Juno stays, haunting the place where his Beloved died.

"Come …" I say, pulling Juno gently away. Time means nothing. We will return here. But we have a million Beloveds to embrace. I need to pull Juno to a place that is happy, where we can be together without the evils of the world tearing us apart.

"Mars, why am I so tired?" Juno asks.

I quiver with excitement. "It is Cesare, your Beloved who is tired, and it is for the best of reasons!" I want Juno to remember on his own. I want him to feel the happiness here, in spite of the tiredness that accompanies it.

"His tiredness is my own. His pain is my own."

"Are you in pain, Juno?" I ask.

"Yes. Pain. In my back, the muscles. I've been carrying a heavy load."

I nudge Ryan, and he reaches out to massage Cesare's aching back. It isn't enough.

Juno is pulled backwards, towards the beginning yet not quite to The Beginning, from which we are severed.

I meet him in Jeremiah.

We wrestle.

I do not want to fight Juno, but a human Beloved cannot reconcile two incorporeum within the same host.

I pull him away.

I pull him away before …

#

"Reuben!" Yissachar whispered harshly. "What is it you are doing? This is not right!"

Reuben spat on the ground. "It is our way. It is our right. Why would they have come to Sodom if they did not want to experience the fullness of our pleasures?" Reuben opened his arms wide, mocking his cousin's reluctance.

"If it is pleasure they seek, they can find it themselves. Please, I beg you, let us return home." Yissachar trotted after his cousin, pulling ineffectually at Reuben's robes. "Our aunt will feed us, and you can sleep off the heavy drink."

Reuben swatted Yissachar's hands away. "I'm not ready to go home yet. Not to our uncle's house, and certainly not to my father in Zoar." He spat the name as if it caused a bad taste in his mouth.

Yissachar trailed after Reuben. The only way he'd convinced Reuben's father to let the cousins go to Sodom was because Yissachar had promised to watch over Reuben. "He just needs some time … away … to expend his youthful energy. I will not leave his side, Uncle, I swear!" Yissachar regretted the part about not leaving Reuben's side.

His cousin was stubborn as a donkey with a head harder than a goat's.

"Hey! You there." Reuben called out to the two young men, obviously visitors. They looked Reuben up and down, then grinned. Yissachar shuddered, hanging back just enough to not cause a confrontation.

"Aha! The legendary hospitality of Sodom, on display," said one of the strangers. He stared, unashamed, at Reuben's groin as he spoke.

Reuben scratched his balls. "Our hospitality knows no bounds," he growled, reaching out to squeeze the man's arm. "Have you rooms for the night?"

Yissachar panicked. Reuben might be in search of the highest form of debauchery he could find, and his father might never find out. But if they failed to return to their uncle's house for the night, the family would do more than worry.

The three of them were touching each other, right there in the open square. The few people who turned to look simply laughed or yelled crude comments, egging them on.

"And your friend?"

"My cousin," Reuben explained. "My self-appointed keeper."

The three of them laughed, then turned towards a nearby inn, talking in voices too low for Yissachar to hear.

"Reuben!" Yissachar called out. "We should be going home to our uncle's house. They will worry about us." Yissachar emphasized the word 'worry,' hoping that his cousin would catch his meaning.

"You go home then and tell them what they can do with themselves. Or with their asses. Or each other's asses, if they aren't already," Reuben called, walking into the Inn with his new friends.

Yissachar followed, but they went into a room and slammed the door in his face. He tried not to think about what was happening inside. He only hoped they would finish quickly, so he could get his cousin home without anyone questioning where they'd been or what they'd been doing.

The innkeeper staunchly ignored the rough sounds coming from the room. Yissachar hovered outside the door. He tried the latch once, but it was locked. He thought about knocking but could not muster the courage to do so.

Suddenly the door was flung open, and the two young men rushed out. They pushed past Yissachar and out into the creeping darkness.

Yissachar peeked into the room, then he heard his cousin groan. A voice inside him whispered *That was not a groan of satisfaction. He is in pain.* With newfound courage, Yissachar stumbled into the room, not being able to see much in the darkened space. The only window was shuttered, and the light outside was quickly fading.

"Reuben?" he called softly.

"Robbed! The bastards robbed me," Reuben said. Yissachar found him curled up in a ball on the floor. "But not before I stuck them both. And they liked it, too! They were already salved and slippery. I'm glad I only had a few coins on me. It would have cost me more to pay a pretty boy to bend over. I just wish they hadn't beaten me to get it." Reuben tried to laugh but ended up coughing.

Yissachar begged a bowl of water and piece of linen from the Innkeeper then helped his cousin clean up. Despite his injuries, Reuben seemed to be in good spirits. It was not easy to find their way home in the dark, but at least when they got there no one seemed to be overly curious about where they'd been all day. Yissachar helped Reuben to bed with the help of one of the servant girls. He cringed when he saw the look of despair and abandonment on her face as he left her alone with Reuben, but there was nothing he could do. That was her place. And if it kept Reuben safely at home, that was all that really mattered.

#

I pull Juno from Reuben, dragging him forward, to the place where we are happy. But he finds Kristophe, and then the absence of Kristophe. Adam is older now. He's outgrowing his tiny bed, but no one seems to notice.

I stay with them both. Juno, incorporeal, hostless, in the corner by the window, mourning Kristophe. Adam, whose loneliness and confusion threaten to overwhelm me.

Adam sleeps, and I pull Juno away, forward again. We pause in many hosts along the way, always together. No matter what human era, Juno and I are always together.

Almost always together.

#

"Come on, Ernest," Scot called from the back of the hay wagon. "You can come, too."

Ernest looked up at the wagon full of young people and hesitated. He desperately wanted to go, but in such close quarters he wouldn't be able to fade into the background so easily.

And there were *girls*.

Women.

Real women.

Gerilyn smiled and held out a hand to help him up. She'd been dating some guy who worked on an oil rig forever. She was probably safe.

Ernest's heart broke as he watched Scot flirt with Gerilyn's cousin, some city girl who was spending the summer on the wild Wyoming plains in what her parents called 'a desperate attempt to break her unhealthy addiction to MTV.'

Fortunately, Gerilyn spent most of the ride defending her cousin from Scot's teasing. Ernest was able to sit back in the corner, as invisible as possible to the rest of the crowd.

When they got to the firepit, Ernest jumped out before the wagon stopped. He ran off to gather firewood, hoping that being useful would mean being accepted, or at least tolerated.

He'd rather be alone with Scot. Here, in this crowd, they couldn't … they couldn't just be themselves.

Being himself was not safe.

#

I always try to make Ernest feel safe, but he is right. He lives with danger, and his life is short.

I don't know what conversations Juno has with Scot. They do converse. Scot knows he is not alone. He calls Juno 'the demon inside.'

I take Juno forward again. If we can only reach the happy place, all will be well, but our happy hosts are tired. It is not the tiredness of a long day's work or of an energetic session of exercise. It is a hopeless, bone-weary kind of tiredness that neither of them has ever experienced. It is something that, although they were warned, they never expected.

Juno falls back, and I must follow.

#

"Scot?" Ernest asked, knocking softly on the old, scratched-up door. "Your mom sent me up. Are you okay?"

"Yeah," Scot grunted, not turning away from the window. Ernest closed the door behind him.

He walked over to the window and looked out over the yard full of chickens. "So, does this mean you're quitting your job in Powell?"

"I called my boss yesterday and explained how my mom can't get by out here on her own now that Dad's gone."

Ernest shuffled his feet, not knowing what to say. They'd all expressed their condolences. They'd stood by the graveside, holding onto their hats as the Wyoming wind threatened to blow them to Nebraska.

Ernest didn't want to think about going on without Scot, but he had no reason to stay with him on the ranch. The only reason he was still around at all was because he was Scot's best friend, but it was the end of the week and there was no longer a good excuse for Ernest to stay.

Except that he was in love with Scot.

Scot sniffed and wiped his face on his sleeve. Ernest had never seen him cry before. Scot had never been close to his father.

Ernest put a hand on Scot's back. "Don't think these tears are for *him*," Scot half growled, half sobbed. "It's just that … I just started my job. It's a place I like, with good people. And now, now I have to come back here, doing every chore I ever resented doing."

Ernest came close and embraced his friend, thumping his back in what he hoped was a manly way. Scot clung to him, wrapping his arms around Ernest and rocking back and forth. Ernest breathed in his scent, wishing that it hadn't taken a death in the family for Scot to finally touch him. Maybe, just maybe, now that the old man was dead, maybe they could have a future together. Ernest's accounting skills might not be vital to the ranch, but they could make some kind of excuse about wanting to hire a business manager or something. Or he could commute.

Ernest's thoughts were disrupted as he realized that Scot was looking down at him. He'd stopped rocking. He was looking at Ernest's mouth.

Ernest had never been kissed. Not by a woman, and certainly not by a man. He trembled, anticipating the moment.

A door slammed downstairs. Scot pushed him away roughly then jumped away and paced in front of the window.

"Back to every chore I ever resented doing," Scot said, as if the moment had never passed between them. "I just don't know how I'm gonna do it. I just don't know."

Ernest knew how he could get through it. They could do it together, if only Scot would let him.

#

As we leave Ernest and Scot, I pull Juno past Kristophe, not wanting to let him linger in the sadness. After sharing Scot's mourning and frustration, I'm afraid of what Juno might do.

We touch various Beloveds as we make our way back, but Juno seeks the sadness now. It tempts him. Whether he feels compelled to stay in these times so that he can bring comfort to his Beloveds or he is hopelessly lost in the illness itself, I do not know.

He wears remorse like a cloak, although we have not yet reached its source.

#

I see the bruises on the servant girl's face and arms, and I make Yissachar notice them too, even though no one else in the house is concerned.

I feel the tiniest tinge of remorse from him. I try to amplify it, to prompt him to action, but he bats me away.

The servant girl is a Beloved of the incorporeum, but this is not the only reason I want to help her. Yissachar's life is short. He needs to do something good before …

Before.

"She is mine tonight," I hear Yissachar say, grabbing the girl and hauling her into his room. Reuben starts yelling, and I hear Juno trying to calm him down, but Reuben is too strong-willed, even for Juno. Sometimes I think Juno's failure with Reuben frustrates him even more than his failure with Scot.

I am ahead of myself. I experience my Beloved's lives as a whole. My Beloveds experience their lives as if ordered in a straight line.

It is strange.

The servant girl huddles in a corner, watching Yissachar undress. When he collapses onto his bed, she goes to him, tentatively. She pauses, looking at the door.

"Will she flee?" I ask her incorporeum.

"No," comes the answer. "It would be worse for her. We will stay."

She touches Yissachar and he turns to look at her. She removes her robe, one shoulder at a time, but Yissachar is not aroused at all. He is only uncomfort-able. "There is no need," he tells her, and she looks surprised. "Just sleep. Over there."

The girl looks confused, but she lies down on a mat as far from Yissachar as she can, and soon they are both asleep.

"Mars?" the other incorporeum asks. "How is it that you and Juno have names? None of us have names. Even calling ourselves 'incorporeum' is no more than a description of *what* we are, not *who* we are. Adam could not see us. Adam did not name us."

I chuckle. "Adam named me Mars, and he named Juno, as well." I do not let the joke linger. "Not Adam of The Garden, Adam my Beloved. He named us."

"I wish Adam would give me a name."

The servant girl's incorporeum sounds wistful. As we speak, I feel her growing closer to me. I know her. I recognize her.

"Come with me!" I say, and I reach for Adam.

#

Adam watched Juno pass through the walls of the old house. He didn't dare tell anyone. At least Juno was no longer confined to the cold corner of Adam's little room. Adam himself was no longer confined to the tiny attic room. He was a grown man.

Adam waited patiently in his chair. He could hear the baby, his new niece. He was eager to see her, but he knew if he left his chair he would do something wrong and they'd lock him in his room. It was a nice room, but Adam didn't want to be alone. Even with Mars and Juno to keep him company, he felt that he would die of loneliness.

So, he behaved.

He sat in his chair.

Finally, his sister appeared, her husband hovering behind her. He was a nice man. Adam thought he was smiling because the corners of his mouth were turned up. But somehow, his face wasn't smiling. Adam had no idea what that meant.

"Adam, meet your new niece—"

"Xenia!" Adam blurted, jumping to his feet.

His sister shushed him, and her husband placed his hands on her shoulders. It was the same way father placed his hands on mother's shoulders when he was about to steer her away—away from Adam.

Adam sat down, his leg bouncing eagerly despite all efforts to calm himself. Mrs was no help. Mars was laughing happily.

The baby was not alone. His niece had an incorporeum! And her name—this was Adam's job—her name was Xenia. For she was hospitable and sweet. She would be the one, she would bring Juno rest.

"You're not going to let him hold her, are you?" whispered Adam's brother-in-law.

"Ah, no," Adam's sister said. "Not yet. Perhaps when she's a little bigger." She leaned over and held the baby so he could see her. "Adam, this is your niece, Eugenia."

"You … genia," Adam said carefully. He wanted to tell his sister about the incorporeum. He wanted her to know how wonderful her daughter's life would be, to have a friend so close at all times, but he knew what would happen if he told.

Adam blew her a kiss. "Sweet baby," he said, making no move to touch her. He'd touched his brother's baby once, and his sister-in-law had collapsed into hysterics, grabbing the baby away.

Adam would behave.

Adam would sit in his chair.

If Adam did everything right, or did nothing at all, Adam would not be lonely.

#

Yissachar did nothing. He stood at the back of the crowd, knowing he was helpless to pull Reuben away.

"Send them out to us!" the crowd roared in unison.

"Have you seen them? They're beautiful!" a man next to him remarked. "They have to come out sooner or later."

Yissachar shook his head. The simple motion conveyed multiple meanings, but the man was no longer looking at him. "Hey! I'll take one of the daughters if no one else wants them!" the man yelled.

Yissachar tried to figure out what had happened. Apparently, the man who was hosting the beautiful strangers had offered to give his daughters to the crowd, but the mob demanded he send out the strangers instead.

A sudden darkness fell over Yissachar's eyes. The crown roared. "What is happening?" cried one.

"Blind! I am blind!" cried another.

"Reuben? Reuben!" Yissachar called, lunging forward, panic overriding sense. He had to find his cousin. He had to make sure he was safe.

Strong arms grabbed him. "Yissachar? What trickery is this?" he asked.

"I, I don't know. Perhaps it is only night, taking us by surprise. We have lost track of time," Yissachar replied. All around them, the crowd was growing unrulier. Yissachar fumbled and dragged his cousin against a wall. They crouched down, Yissachar shielding Reuben, while men stumbled and cursed the darkness all around them.

Hours passed. They were kicked a few times, but it was only others in the crowd tripping over them as they yelled and screamed and tried to find their way in the strange darkness.

"Yissachar?" Reuben asked.

"Yes, Reuben?"

"I have not made my family proud."

Yissachar shook his head, even though Reuben couldn't see him. "You're no different from most young men. You just need to sow some wild oats."

"No. No, I'm worse. Or, I want to be worse. Inside, I know I am evil. I cannot hide it. I tried everything I could to … to be vile. To show them the darkness within me. Yet no matter how debauched, how cruel, there is always someone to say 'You think that's bad? Just watch this!' Then they do something even worse. I can't … I can't be wicked enough. I was terrible at being good, but I'm worse at being evil."

Yissachar had nothing to say. He was afraid of his cousin's confession and afraid of the darkness. He fumbled for his wineskin, relieved to find it was still half full. "Here, drink," he said.

Reuben drank.

Reuben slept.

A light appeared. Yissachar wasn't sure if it was dawn, a reflection of something, or just his mind playing tricks on him.

The light grew large, and with it came a heat so intense Yissachar feared he would be burned alive.

But fire was not to be their fate.

It was the impact that ended their mortal existence.

#

"And God rained fire and brimstone down upon the cities of Sodom and Gomorrah, destroying the evil Sodomites for their wicked ways …"

The preacher went on and on, elaborating on the abomination of homosexuality and how it was the one unforgivable sin. Ernest sat next to Scot in the crowded pew. He was sure everyone knew. They must be able to see the connection between them, even though they'd never shared anything more intimate than a hug.

When Ernest saw his own reflection with Scot, all he could think of was how perfect they were together. But that was only when they were alone. And even alone, Scot would never admit to being one of *those* people.

They stuffed their faces at Scot's mother's house, thanked her, and loaded the dishwasher. With the minimal requirements of civility thus disposed of, they were out the front door and down the road before she could nag them about anything else that needed to be done.

It was Sunday. A day of rest.

"You did not!" Ernest said, punching Scot in the arm as they followed the railroad tracks.

Scot laughed. Ernest loved hearing that laugh. He imagined it was for his ears only. After all, the only time Scot truly laughed was when the two of them were alone. If anyone else was around, all Scot would do was humph or let out a manly snort.

"I did too. Right in front of her big brother, too," Scot said. He turned toward Ernest, putting his hands on Ernest's hips. "I took her in my arms ..." Ernest's arms found their way to Scot's shoulders, as if it was the most natural thing in the world to do. "I leaned in, and I ..."

Scot was leaning in. Ernest was looking up into his gorgeous brown eyes.

Scot kissed him. For a moment, Ernest's heart sang in perfect happiness.

The happiness was shattered when Scot pushed him away.

"Well, I kissed her better than that," Scot said, spitting onto the rails and wiping his mouth on his sleeve. He wasn't looking at Ernest. He was hurrying away.

It was not how Ernest had imagined their first kiss.

He should follow Scot's lead, and just laugh it off. But, something inside him refused to let go of the hope.

He stayed put on the rails, exactly where he'd been standing when their lips touched.

Scot looked back. "What the hell are you doing?"

Ernest spread his arms wide. "I've waited my whole life for that! And I'm not letting it go so easily."

It was the bravest thing he'd ever done. It was a risk, but there was no one around to see. There was no one around to judge.

"Waited for what?" Scot said, looking off down the tracks. He kicked at the dirt.

"You know what? You kissed me."

"I was joking! It was just a dumb story. Geez, you can't just—"

"You kissed me, Scot. Because you wanted to," Ernest said. He wasn't going to let go. He couldn't just do *nothing*. He couldn't go on pretending they were just friends, watching the man he loved tumble one girl after another, trying to prove to everyone how much of a man he was.

Ernest shifted his weight, letting his boot slip down where the rails split off to the east. His boot wedged itself in tightly, but it didn't matter. Ernest was standing his ground. Scot would have to admit he loved him, or he'd stay rooted to that very spot forever.

"Don't be stupid," Scot said, turning his back again.

A rumble sounded in the distance. Ernest could feel the vibrations in the rails. Still, he stood his ground.

"Get back up here," he said, his voice more authoritative than it had ever been in his entire life. The kiss empowered him. All the near misses they'd had … but the kiss …

He knew Scot had feelings for him. Feelings that ran far deeper than friendship.

Scot was hunched over, strangely diminished. He kicked at the dirt, refusing to look up. "Don't be stupid, Ernest," he said, his eyes meeting Ernest's for just a fleeting second.

This was Ernest's chance to be resilient. All his life, Scot had been the strong one. Scot had stood up for him, watched over him. But Scot wasn't brave enough for this one thing, this one declaration.

"I love you, Scot," Ernest said.

Finally, Scot looked up. Their eyes met and Ernest reached out his hand.

A whistle blew in the distance.

Scot stood straight again. "All right. You love me. Now get down from there."

Ernest shook his head. "Not until you tell me you love me, too."

Scot kicked a rock, wincing as it unintentionally flew close by Ernest's head.

Ernest just smiled. "Come on. No one else needs to know, Scot, but I need to hear it. I know you love me, but I need to hear it from your own mouth."

The chugging sound that had been no more than a rumble was now audible. Ernest shifted his weight and discovered that his foot was wedged tighter than he thought. It was stuck.

"What the—" Ernest pulled at his boot, but he couldn't free it or get his foot out.

"Stop messing around, Ernest, the train's coming!" Scot said, coming to him at last.

Ernest started to panic. "I'm not fooling, Scot, my foot's stuck!"

Scot came up on the tracks with him, his strong, sure arms steadying him. He crouched, twisting Ernest's foot.

Then he stopped.

"Ernest," he said, his eyes full of fear. Ernest didn't know if it was fear of his own emotions or of the train, or both. He wished he could freeze the moment in time. He was sure Scot was about to tell him he loved him, too.

Scot didn't say anything. He jerked at Ernest's ankle a few more times then braced himself as if he was about to lift Ernest right out of his boots. That might work if he could get straight up. Scot was a big guy. He could do it.

Scot stopped. He looked down the tracks. Ernest could feel the train getting close, just beyond the curve. The conductor wouldn't see them until he was almost on them. There was no stopping a train.

Scot looked Ernest in the eyes. Time stood still.

"Ernest, I love you," Scot said, locking eyes. "But it's better this way."

Scot tumbled to the side just as the train roared down on them.

#

"I'm sorry," whispers Juno from the end of Adam's bed. It is a big, comfortable bed, but the door is still locked. Adam is still stuck in his room.

"Sorry for what?" I ask.

"Scot … is sorry for Ernest," Juno says.

"Oh," I say. "I know."

"And—," Juno says. Adam is asleep. I'm glad. He would not want to hear the things we speak of.

"And Reuben—" Juno cannot finish the sentence.

"Reuben was passed out drunk when it happened," I remind him.

"Yissachar would not have been in Sodom if it wasn't for Reuben."

"Juno, do you have control over any of your Beloveds?"

Juno thinks about that. I know he wants to take responsibility. He yearns for redemption on their behalf. "I … influence them."

I sigh. "Perhaps you have some influence, but you love unconditionally, do you not?"

Juno shrugs. Or at least, what I know is a shrug. Being incorporeal, it's hard to tell.

"It is our way," he says.

Unconditional love is indeed our way. But so is forgiveness.

"And Jeremiah?" Juno asks.

"What of Jeremiah?" I ask.

"Did he die because of me?"

I embrace my friend. I would pull him into Adam with me if that was possible. "Juno, Jeremiah died by his own hand. I do not know why we were both pulled into him. It was not meant to be that way."

We are quiet for a while. Distantly, Adam's infant niece cries.

Juno leaps, and he is gone. I know where he has gone, though. I know that Xenia is waiting for him to recognize her.

I will not leave Adam, not even while he sleeps. But a moment later, Juno returns.

"Mars!" he says.

I smile and wait.

"Is it—"

"Yes, Juno. We should go there."

I do not have to pull Juno. This time, he knows. This time, he remembers.

"Cesare?" Juno asks, settling down into his Beloved as I settle into mine. "But, we are so tired."

"Yes, and Reuben was tired. He was tired of living the way he lived, of no one caring. He tried to care even less, but that was not possible."

"And Scot?" Juno asks.

"Scot was tired of pretending to be someone he was not. He saw his own future. He saw that he would have to go on pretending forever. He could not stand to face that."

"And Cesare?" Juno asks.

Xenia calls to us. "Juno! Let Cesare wake up. He has to wake up."

Juno hesitates. His instinct is to soothe his Beloved, to help Cesare sleep.

I nudge Ryan's mind to wakefulness, even though he is just as tired as Cesare.

Cesare rouses and reaches out to embrace Ryan. He gives his husband a kiss on the cheek. "No, darling, you rest. I'll get her."

I feel Ryan's grateful mind slip back into peaceful slumber. Cesare gets out of bed. Juno is remembering now. He is remembering why we are tired.

He is also remembering why we are happy.

"We are wet, and we are hungry!" Xenia yells. I laugh.

"Here, sweetling, come to Daddy," Cesare croons, picking up the baby. Xenia sighs with relief.

"Somebody needs a new diaper!"

I can feel Juno letting go. He lets go of his remorse for Jeremiah. He lets go of his grief for Kristophe. He lets go of his guilt over Reuben and Scot.

He embraces his daughter.

Our daughter.

And we are free.

OMEGA

IN THE SHALLOWS

John Vicary

There is a sea in faraway Israel where nothing grows. It is called the Dead Sea, although it was not always known as such. In ancient times, it was invoked in many tongues, but most often it was named *Yām ha-Mizrahî*: the Eastern Sea.

A man may lie in the less famous shallows of the sister of the Sea of Galilee and rise to the top without effort, buoyed to the surface by science or faith. He need only to gaze upon its barren shores to delineate the foothills of history, when other men may have tried to float in the same sea and failed the test. How much does man trust in his knowledge and how much does he heed the pull of those stories from his youth? The joy drains from that swim like water from a cracked vessel, and he wonders if he had lived at that time in this land of Canaan if he would have escaped the brimstone fate that awaited so many others. His gaze traces the horizon and a twinge gnaws his gut. The sheltering arms of the waves remind him of a different embrace in years already spent.

Two angels had descended from heaven to give warning to the righteous, his mother had told him long ago. He could still hear her voice as she told him her favorite biblical tale.

"Disguised as two men, the angels tried to pass Lot's house on their way to Sodom, but he insisted they break bread with him," Mama said. "In those times,

it was a solemn duty to give hospitality to those in need."

"I'd recognize them, Mama," he said. He imagined the men with a certain golden glow or perhaps an errant feather peeking from under their cloaks. "I'm special."

"Of course, you are, sweetie," she answered, pulling the blanket up to his chest as she readied him for bed. "But there's no way to know by looking. That's why it's always important to be kind, especially to strangers. Maybe you'll be talking to an angel all along."

If he wouldn't recognize angels for who they were, would he heed their warning when it came? Would they even consider him worth warning, or would they let him burn like the five cities of the plain? He hugged his bear to his chest. "Are angels ever bad, Mama?"

"Why would you think such a thing?" Mama brushed the hair from his

forehead. "Sodom and Gomorrah were destroyed because the people were wicked. You have nothing to fear if you follow God's path."

"But Mama, didn't those people think they were on God's path?" he asked. "They didn't want to be killed by angels. They didn't want to die, did they?"

Mama frowned. "Of course not. They weren't killed by angels, but by God himself. You're too young to understand. Go to sleep now and forget these questions. You'll give yourself nightmares."

A man might still remember nightmares of his boyhood: they had been full of ash and smoke and skin peeling from blistered bone. Some nights he is plagued with sulfur dreams from the archaic demolition of the disgraced cities of Canaan. He imagines the angels standing sentinel in the Hebron Hills over the lava that buries the screaming sinners. He blinks and is somewhat surprised to find himself not amongst that mass ruination but floating safe in present waters.

"But, Mama, didn't the people think they were on God's path?"

His mother had never wanted to answer that question, and he'd stopped asking. He'd ceased wondering about morals or angels or people from the past, even if his nightmares hadn't given up their grip on his subconscious quite as easily.

"I'd recognize them. I'm special."

Special.

The thoughts, or perhaps the desert sun, grow too warm for comfort, and the man rises from the murky water. He's had enough of the sea.

As he brushes loose the salt that has dried into a crust on his body, another pilgrim wanders from the water. "I'm glad I could be here to swim in the sea before it disappears, aren't you?"

The man says nothing.

"Many people don't realize that it's disappearing," the pilgrim says. "But it is, you know. Faster every day, it seems."

"No, I didn't know," the man says.

The pilgrim sifts through his backpack and withdraws a canteen. He offers it to the man.

The man pushes it away with a curt shake of his head.

"Meanwhile, Mount Sodom continues to grow in size," the pilgrim says before taking a drink.

"What?" the man asks. The brine stings his eyes, and he rubs at them. The pilgrim is a blur in his vision.

"That mountain," the pilgrim continues, pointing to the opposite shore. "It's made entirely of halite. Salt. It's been growing for thousands of years. Hence the name. It's from the biblical city. See that little pillar that's separated from the rest, just there?"

The man squints in the bright light, his eyes still tearing. "Oh, yes. I see it."

"It's called Lot's Wife. You can explore the formation if you'd like. It's growing at an amazing rate. They say that if you stand in the salt caves at midnight, you can see your salvation." The pilgrim caps his water and rises to stand.

The man frowns. "I don't understand. What does that mean?"

The pilgrim shrugs. "It's a tradition. I've heard that people see all sorts of things. Maybe you'll try it. What do you suppose you'll see?"

The man considers it for a moment. He closes his near-sightless eyes and pictures the smooth walls of Mount Sodom surrounding him in the desert heat. The passage narrows to a squeeze, and he tips his chin north—the only free space in the enclosure—to find his salvation. He's waited for this forever, it seems. He's wondered how he is different from those people who God saw fit to burn in this very spot. He has questioned how, exactly, he is so special. He wants to see an angel waiting just for him, but he fears he wouldn't recognize the face of one even if God saw fit to grace him with a messenger. The truth is that he is no different from the people who were cursed to die by fire. He fears, above all, he would open his eyes in that salt cave to see nothing but the clear night sky stretching out above him into an unanswered oblivion.

"I wouldn't see anything," the man says.

"Are you sure?" the pilgrim asks. He cocks his head. "It's a special place, if you open your eyes."

"Maybe for some." The man blinks to clear his blurred vision and pulls his shirt over his head. "I saw what I came for."

He walks to his car. On his way, he throws away his brochure extolling the healing wonders of the Dead Sea. He hadn't liked his visit as much as he'd expected to. Vacations were supposed to be fun, not filled with fear of fire. Maybe the next destination would be more enjoyable.

He drives away without looking back, but the figure of the pilgrim limns his rearview. The last of the salt washes clear from his eyes just as the rays of the setting sun grace the edge of the Masada ridge. By a trick of the evening light, it seems as if the pilgrim is beyond radiant. The man pulls to the side of the road to get a better view of the spectacle, but by the time he exits the car the sun has already set and there is no sign of anyone behind him. He is alone in the road in the dark with only the endless sky above him. He regrets that he didn't try harder to see his salvation when the glimpse was offered. Now he has lost the chance. The man looks up and sighs. The first star of the night appears. It is beautiful to behold.

BIOS

Alexander, Terry and his wife Phyllis live on a small farm near Porum, Oklahoma. They have three children, thirteen grandchildren, and eight great grandchildren. Terry has been published in various anthologies from Airship 27, OGHMA Creative Media, Pro Se Productions, and Pulp Cult. He is a member of the Tahlequah Writers, Oklahoma Writers Federation, Ozark Writers League, and Western Fictioneers.

Anderson, David lives in Mesa, Arizona and makes his living doing art and design. His fiction has appeared in *Surreal Grotesque*, *Bizarrro Central*, Jason Wayne Allen's Rotgut County Blog, and Dynatox Minstries. This April saw the release of his first print collection, "Yakuza Cereal."

Beacham, C.J. writes fiction that has been described as "dark yet hopeful." His short stories have been published by New Lit Salon Press and Santa Fe Writer's Project (under the name Charles J. Beacham). He is a member of The Writer's Workshop of Asheville. C.J. Beacham writes from the foothills of North Georgia where he is working on a second novel and a short story collection while seeking publication for his first novel. He can be found online at https://www.facebook.com/CJBeachamwriter.

Cianci, J.P. is a senior at UNLV studying for a B.A. in English with a concentration in Creative Writing. With a B.S. in Business, she is a member of the Association of Writers and Writing Programs and writes for UNLV's *Rebel Yell*.

DeHart, JD has been publishing for two decades. His work has appeared in *AIM*, *Modern Dad*, and *Steel Toe Review*. When he is not writing, he teaches English.

De Marco, Guy is a speculative fiction author; a Graphic Novel Bram Stoker and Scribe Award finalist; winner of the HWA Silver Hammer Award; a prolific short story and flash fiction crafter; a novelist; a poet; an invisible man with superhero powers; a game writer; and a coffee addict. One of these is false. A writer since 1977, Guy is or has been a member of SFWA, IAMTW, ITW, RWA-PRO, WWA, SFPA, ASCAP, MWG, SWG, HWA, and IBPA. He hopes to collect the rest of the alphabet one day. Learn more about Guy De Marco at his website, GuyAnthonyDeMarco.com, and on Wikipedia at en.wikipedia.org/wiki/Guy_Anthony_De_Marco.

De Marco, Tonya is a costume designer, professional cosplayer, published model, and author. She lives in a cabin in the woods in rural Ohio. She's been hooked on costumes and costuming since she was a preteen. She's been featured in several magazines and on the GeekxGirls website. Additionally, her love of the written word encouraged her to pursue a writing career. Tonya has numerous short stories in anthologies and is a member of the Horror Writers Association. When she isn't sewing or writing, Tonya enjoys spending time listening to the silence of the forest. Visit her website at http://www.TonyaLDeMarco.com to find links to her Facebook, Instagram, and Amazon accounts.

Eden, Meg teaches creative writing at colleges and writing centers. She is the author of the 2021 Towson Prize for Literature winning poetry collection *Drowning in the Floating World* (Press 53, 2020) and children's novels, most recently *Good Different*, a JLG Gold Standard selection (Scholastic, 2023). Find her online at https://linktr.ee/medenauthor.

Hewitt, Gary enjoys both prose and poetry. His many stories and poems, which venture into the quirky and mysterious, have been published online and offline. His style has adapted over the years. These days he enjoys experimenting with unusual formats. He lives in the UK and is currently studying German. He's not going to Germany but figured it'll keep his mind active. He continues to write and has read his work publicly, which was fun even if a touch nerve wracking. He also enjoys tarot and reiki and loves to hear feedback from fans. His website is located at https://kingsraconteurswork.blogspot.com.

Inverness, AmyBeth AmyBeth Inverness is a historian and writer who takes inspiration from the realities and unknowns of humanity to write thought-provoking speculative fiction. She lives in the basement of a historic Denver mansion with her cat and a mostly harmless set of unidentifiable entities. You can find her stories in all the BLAS books and in the back of a desk drawer where they ferment like kombucha awaiting an audience with a suitable palate. Samples of both her millinery and fiction can be found at http://amybethinverness.com/.

Morehouse, Lyda leads a double life. By day she's a mild-mannered science fiction author of such works as the Shamus Award-winning and Locus Award-nominated *Archangel Protocol* (2001.) By night, she dons her secret identity as Tate Hallaway, best-selling paranormal romance author. Her most recent novel, *Unjust Cause*, was published by Wizard Tower Press in April 2020. You can find her all over the Web as Lyda Morehouse, and at Twitter as @tatehallaway. Be sure to check out what she's been up to lately at https://lydamorehouse.com and https://www.patreon.com/lydamorehouse.

Paschall, Nicholas is a horror and fantasy author based out of Texas, where he lives with his wife, cats, and dog. He was first published in 2011 and has since been published in over fifty anthologies, magazines, and ezines. His first novel, the *Father of Flesh*, was published in 2017 with a sequel released a year later. He spends most of his time crawling the internet looking for inspiration for his next tale of terror.

Rose, Rie Sheridan has prose published in numerous anthologies, including *Killing It Softly Vols. 1 & 2*, *Hides the Dark Tower*, *Dark Divinations*, and *Startling Stories*. Additionally, she has authored twelve novels in multiple genres, six poetry chapbooks, and dozens of song lyrics. She is a native of Texas and lives there with her husband and several spoiled cats, though they hope to move to Dublin, Ireland in the future. When not writing or editing, she is usually walking and being a Virtual Race addict. Member of the HWA and SFWA, she tweets as @RieSheridanRose.

Varga, Kris Twenty-three years old. Six feet tall, blonde hair, blue eyes, slender frame, long face, protruding nose, Caucasian. A graduate of the studies at Temple University in Film and Media Arts. He also possesses a minor in English Literature. Rambunctious poet. Actor. Musician. Film Editor. Friend.

Vataris, Erin is a freelance short fiction writer currently working on several speculative fiction and post-apocalyptic collections. Her short story "Mote" is included in the Garden of Eden anthology through Garden Gnome Publications. She has never beaten her children for being afraid of the dark. She can be found on <u>Google Plus</u>.

Vicary, John began publishing poetry in the fifth grade and has been writing ever since. A contributor to many compendiums, his most recent credentials include short fiction in the collections "The Longest Hours," "Midnight Circus," "Something's Brewing," and "Temporary Skeletons." He has stories in upcoming issues of *Disturbed Digest* and "Dead Men's Tales." John enjoys playing piano and lives in rural Michigan with his family. You can read more of his work at <u>keppiehed.com</u>.

Wynn, E.S. is the author of over seventy books and the chief editor of Thunderune Publishing. In his spare time, he spins stories, builds board games, stitches together battle jackets, runs a pair of magazines, makes videos about Norse Shamanism on YouTube, and encourages people to create new art. He is openly transgender and seeks to establish acceptance and love for and within the trans community. He has worked with hundreds of authors and edited thousands of manuscripts for nearly a dozen different magazines. His stories and articles have been published in dozens of journals, e-zines, and anthologies. He has taught classes in literature, marketing, math, spirituality, energetic healing, and guided meditation, and he has worked as a voice-over artist for several horror and sci-fi podcasts, albums, and e-books.

Zimmermann, Melchior interrupted his master's thesis in biology to work for a year as a substitute teacher. He recently moved to Amsterdam to spend more time on the arts, especially writing. He likes to experiment with different genres and content. You can read more of his writing at <u>behindthez.blogspot.com</u>.

ABOUT THE EDITOR

Allen Taylor is the publisher at <u>Garden Gnome Publications</u> and editor of the Biblical Legends Anthology Series. His fiction and poetry have been published online and in print. He is the author of two non-fiction books on the intersection between cryptocurrency and social media as well as a spiritual testimony titled *I Am Not the King*, all available at <u>Amazon</u>. He is the creator of the #twitpoem hashtag at Twitter and writes a <u>newsletter/blog at Paragraph</u>. He is a freelance writer and book editor at <u>Taylored Content</u>.

LEAVE US A REVIEW

If you liked _Sulfurings: Tales from Sodom and Gomorrah_, the editor and the authors would sincerely invite you to write a review at Amazon, Goodreads, or wherever you purchased this book.

And we thank you from the bottom of our hearts, as do the garden gnomes.

Also look at _Garden of Eden_, the first book in the Biblical Legends Anthology Series, and Deluge: Stories of Survival & Tragedy in the Great Flood.

Please report errors in this e-book to the editor at editor@gardengnomepubs.com.

CONNECT WITH THE GNOMES

The garden gnomes would sincerely like to connect with you at our social media outposts. Please, drop on by!

Follow our editor on <u>Twitter</u>, <u>Hive</u>, and <u>Paragraph</u>.

Books By Allen Taylor

Garden of Eden

The first book in the Biblical Legends Anthology Series, *Garden of Eden* is a multi-author anthology that explores themes related to the creation story. Not Christian but not anti-Christian.

An excerpt from a reader review:

> To answer the obvious question first, while some of the contributors might be Christian, this is not a Christian book; nor is it an attack on Christianity. The works, some more than others, do raise issues of morality and sin, but they are neither thinly veiled allegory nor brutal parody.

Sulfurings: Tales from Sodom & Gomorrah

The second book in the Biblical Legends Anthology Series, *Sulfurings: Tales from Sodom & Gomorrah* is more horrific and apocalyptic than *Garden of Eden*. It also includes more stories from a more diverse group of authors.

From a reader review:

> While *Garden of Eden* was almost lighthearted in its biblical
> fiction, *Sulfurings* was much darker, and gritty. The details of the
> horrors were almost palatable. At times, I imagined I could smell
> the sulfur and feel the terror of those of Sodom. I almost felt
> sorry for them, almost.

Deluge: Stories of Survival & Tragedy in the Great Flood

The third book in the Biblical Legends Anthology Series. *Deluge: Stories of Survival & Tragedy in the Great Flood* takes a weirder turn than the *Garden of Eden* and *Sulfurings*, but the quality of the writing is superb. It also seems to be an audience favorite.

Check out this excerpt from a reader review:

> I have a lot of respect for the work of the editor of this multi-author volume of deluge-related stories. Mr. Taylor has gone to a lot of work to put it together. All the stories and poetic prose in this book are excellent work.

I Am Not the King

I Am Not the King is Allen Taylor's Christian testimony. Beginning with childhood, he details the events while growing up in a legalistic Holiness environment with a father dealing with angry issues and how that impacted his life as a young man. With a stunning twist, he tells how an atheist college professor drove him back to Jesus and what living as a Christian for 30 years has taught him about forgiveness and grace.

An excerpt from a reader review:

> Allen's recognition of the miseries and worldly woes and wrongdoing is the starting point for his search for his real life. This is the story of his search and rescue history. His scathing descriptions of family members, his parents and others, paint large an in-your-face, no-holds-barred, no-punches-pulled, full-frontal exposure of what it's like to be lost with no guidance in the worldly world, always searching for something, something to grasp hold of and hold onto, something solid, something worthy of his trust.

Cryptosocial: How Cryptocurrencies Are Changing Social Media

Written for a general audience, *Cryptosocial: How Cryptocurrencies Are Changing Social Media* details the history of the World Wide Web to illustrate its decentralized beginnings and helps readers understand the basics of blockchain technology and cryptocurrencies. With that understanding, he goes on to detail the growing number of social media platforms where participants can earn cryptocurrencies for their postings.

An excerpt from a reader review:

> While the reality of a decentralized social media is the hope of many people who are concerned—or fed up—with the unchecked clout and excessive influence of legacy media and behemoths like Facebook, Google, and Twitter, the path to decentralization won't be easy. Even so, the book strikes a balance between caution and optimism.

Web3 Social: How Creators Are Changing the World Wide Web (And You Can Too!)

Web3 Social: How Creators Are Changing the World Wide Web (And You Can Too!) is written for the creator class to illustrate how the creator economy is expanding with new monetization protocols, the ability to protect intellectual property and digital identities using blockchain tools, and how creators are going direct to their fans by building their own platforms with Web3 tools of decentralization.

From a reader review:

> As someone who is a four-time self-published author right here on Amazon, and who is old enough now to look back at years on both centralized and decentralized social media and compare, the rightness of this book is perfectly apparent to me. I simply do not want to have my creative life controlled by people who see me only as a chattel. Mr. Taylor shows us creatives the way out of that entrapment.